LAST LAUGH, LAST CRY

WRITTEN BY XANTHE
JOLANDA JOHNSON

Library of Congress Cataloging-in-Publication Data

Johnson, Jolanda Xanthe
Last Laugh, Last Cry
p. cm
Includes index.

ISBN13: 978-1-934947-03-6
LCCN: 2001012345

1. Relationships Fiction 2. Women Fiction. 3. Drama Fiction. I. Title

Any familiarity with characters, and plots in this book are coincidental. All characters are fictitious as well as events.

Printed in the United States of America

BIOGRAPHY

Xanthe pronounced "Zandy" is an aspiring writer who resides currently in Atlanta, Georgia migrating from Florida three years ago.

She is the eldest of five siblings, which includes an identical twin sister. She has one son and one grandson.

Her passion for writing is "an innate gift"; where as she accredits and is grateful to, "My Heavenly Father."

"I believe God blesses each and every one of us with special, unique talents that solidifies our destiny and purpose for life." "It is up to us to embrace the intricacy, which will ultimately ensure a favorable end for us in every dimension of our lives."

Please be sure to check out Xanthe's pursuit for "her favorable end," as she launches her debut book, "LAST LAUGH, LAST CRY," to hit stores in 2009, as she deems, "My year of Divine Completion"... SMOOCHES!

ACKNOWLEDGEMENT

My Heavenly Father.........

Thank you for your immaculate love, grace, and mercy !

Thank you for not letting me "die in the wilderness!"

Thank you for keeping me, disciplining me, redeeming, and resurrecting me!

Thank you for my dreams, and making provisions for them to come to fruition.

Thank you for my family, and my friends whom supported and encouraged me through out this journey.

Thank you for NEVER, EVER LEAVING, NOR FORSAKING ME!

Xanthe

Thank You, Aarika, Bridget, Kim and Natasha!

Smooches!

LAST LAUGH, LAST CRY

WRITTEN BY XANTHE J, JOHNSON

IN MEMORY OF MY FRIEND PATRICIA BONNER...

Patricia, my sweet, beautiful, intelligent, articulate, classy sister. I love you, and miss you!

I see your STAR gleaming in the Heavens with our FATHER.

Your glow, it assures me that you are ok.

I see a yellow rose, and I think of your illuminating smile.

You are and always will be "MY GIRL," and you have indeed had the LAST LAUGH...and certainly your LAST CRY.....

Smooches!
LOVE ME.

LAST LAUGH, LAST CRY

WRITTEN BY XANTHE J. JOHNSON

This book was birthed out of my pain, my healing, my tears, guilt, rejection, humiliation, insanity, sanity, brokenness, wholeness, regrets, falling, and then rising, purity, and the greatest of them all LOVE.

I dedicate this book to my three sisters with much love and admiration. Here's to my special half, but certainly whole in her individual being, **Xanthea; Mija**; when I grow up I'd like to be some of what you are, and **Miko**, you had to have been here on earth before! You are truly an amazing being.

I love and cherish all three of you in my own personal, special way, and thank God you are my Sisters!

My mother **Theadosia-**Thank you for your being you, which made me, ME.

I also dedicate this book to the *"Wind Beneath My Wings"*…. I know you know who you are…but for the sake of the readers of this book….**Dennis Jr. and Dennis III (Boobie), AND Daphne thank you for my grandson!**

Much love for my brothers **Freddie** and **Kyler!** I am so immensely proud of you both! **Kyler**, I would have to write a book to articulate my genuine awe, and how proud I am of you, and perhaps I will!

Freddie, embrace God's plan and desire for your life! Go get your inheritance*!*

CHAPTER ONE

"Raquel, please don't do this. Please, you gon' kill me, man? I don't believe you are doing this to me Raquel! Damn!"

I finally had Daniel Blake Sr. right where I wanted! Now it was time for him to pay for everything he'd ever done to me!

I just sat there so cool, calm, and collected, staring into his deceitful, selfish, evil eyes. He looked like an "old wannabe," a "dropshot," as my sisters would say. A tired, disheveled, old dog; that's what he looked like!

I, on the other hand, look damn good, especially to be a 40-year old grandmother of a two-year old boy. I had lost weight; vigorously working out daily, wearing an amazing size eight. My red Chanel two-piece pantsuit was fitting me well too! I had on the matching hat, shoes, and was sporting the purse too! I even had on white silk Chanel gloves. I just hope I don't splatter any of *his* infectious blood on them! My hair was fly, everything in place, and definitely a pocket full of money! I always had class and style. I *thought* Daniel, Sr. had class, too, until his "ghetto women" started emerging, and their children.

I was a multi-millionaire now! Thanks to the Florida Lottery! That's how I lured Daniel Sr. here. I had devised a plan to consummate his sorry ass, and I was going to get the last laugh. I knew he had heard about me winning the lottery, and it was just a matter of time before this serpent would come crawling for a bite. He had tried fiercely to get in contact with me right after the news hit, just like I knew he would. I refused all attempts he made, until he finally gave up, for a while. There was no way that I was going to give this leech anything, and I was not going to allow any opportunity for him to sojourn back into my life and use me again! I did not even trust myself, because he was my number one demon of temptation.

Daniel Blake Sr. was my first love and my son's father. We met when I was 15 years old at a community dance in our hometown of Tampa, Florida. He was 16. Daniel Sr. was so fine with his creamy complexion, fresh hair cut, and always sporting the latest fashion trends. He had the most beautiful brown eyes, and white teeth. It was evident that his grooming practices were held in high esteem. His cologne was intoxicating, as well as his personality, and I was in *love* instantly. Daniel Sr.'s confidence exuded, which made him very popular with the girls.

I was a sophomore in high school, an above average student, attractive, and pretty popular with my teachers and peers. Most of my popularity stemmed from the fact that I had an identical twin sister, Rachel. We were referred to as "those light-skinned twins with the pretty dimples."

Every one knew of Raquel and Rachel because we shared the same chromosomes; however, unique personalities. Rachel was more of a no-nonsense type, and just took everything so serious. I, on the other hand was much more personable and tolerable than Rachel, except if you crossed me. That would deviate me from you. It may not happen immediately; however, subconsciously you meant nothing to me! You would pay ultimately! Even with the contrast with Rachel and I personalities, we were extremely close and always had each other's back.

Daniel Sr. was not in school at that time. He had been kicked out three months prior for habitual infractions. So, he became a juvenile delinquent, and supported himself from "the streets."

I got pregnant when I was 16 years old, and gave birth to Daniel Jr. nine months later. Daniel Sr. was 17 years old, in and out of the juvenile system, and eventually graduated to the adult system.

I went through hell with him for ten years, although he was in prison for at least five of those years. He was always cheating on me, jumping on me, and disrespecting me. Any good times we shared were virtually forgotten because of all the bad. We were always arguing and fighting about his cheating on me. He was always a dog! He never did anything for me, and not enough for our son. Yet I loved him, and remained faithful to him.

CHAPTER TWO

Daniel Sr. was so shocked when I had "my boys" drag his tired ass out of my bed and "whip" him like *he* was a little boy.

"My boys" were Sergio and Patrick. I had met them in Paris, France a year ago, while I was there to partake in some real estate investments. Sergio was vacationing, and Patrick was there for business. I had been seeking a couple of bodyguards to add to my staff. Both men had come highly recommended to me from my attorney, Janelle. "They are the best in the business," per Janelle. So, I set up private meetings with each of the men, and did some research on each of them myself.

Sergio was from Puerto Rico. A fine Puerto Rican, six feet, body out of this world! He was very attractive, and I sensed a bit of admiration from him to me. We flirted a little with each other, but I had a firm rule about mixing business with pleasure. I think he respected that about me.

Sergio had taught me to speak a little conversational Spanish, and I must say, I was doing "muy bien!" Sergio did not talk much, but did a lot of observing and meditating. I could always count on him, no matter what. He was very loyal and I trusted him to perfect whatever job I paid him well to do.

Patrick was from Brazil. He was very methodical. All had to be in order and on time. His sexy Brazilian accent was confident and authoritative. He was definitely about business. Patrick's expertise was weapons. His knowledge about various types of guns and their components was very impressive.

Sergio and Patrick exceeded the credentials and qualities I was looking for, and I offered each a position on my staff with an excellent salary and benefit package. I was so pleased when Patrick and Sergio both graciously accepted my proposals.

It felt good watching Sergio and Patrick whip Daniel Sr.'s ass, and it felt even better hearing him beg for his life! I had instructed them to whip his skinny ass with a belt too, just like he used to whip me with one, when I would confront him with his whorish escapades.

Daniel Sr. used to jump on me, because *he* was the one screwing around on me! He wanted to do what he wanted to do and continued to cheat on me, but would not allow me to proceed with my life! If he had even heard of me talking with any other guys, it would infuriate him, and of course a confrontation between us ensued.

Many times our son, Daniel Jr., witnessed his father and I turmoil. This affected him tremendously. He unfortunately inherited some of his father's genes; however, he did inherit *my* intellect and creativity. I knew that someday he would use *it*, as he should. Daniel Jr. was just like his father, in so many ways, but I had hope; he did have some of *me* in him. I had faith that part of him would prevail, and by God's grace and mercy, it did!

Daniel Sr. cheated with several women while he was with me, and as a result, two of them, had babies from him. Well at least, he claimed the fame. He *loved* the ghetto, loud mouth, scandalous, illiterate, no class women. Women whom I never would have thought that he would be affiliated with. It was quite embarrassing to me, too, when I would hear rumors about *what* he was messing with now.

Daniel Sr. had always liked younger women. He was so immature and never on my level. The women he dated all still lived at home. None were in school or worked. He was definitely a "paymaster." He took care of his women *and* their entire families.

At the age of 25, Daniel Sr. begin selling drugs and was known as "one of the biggest drug dealers in our town." I imagine he was; he had plenty of women, cars, clothes, and jewelry, but he never gave me a damn thing. All he had ever done was take from me!

I had been out on my own since I was 17 years old, and always had a job. I finished school, continued my education, and maintained a place to stay for my son and I.

While Daniel Sr and I were together, he never paid one of my bills. He never contributed to my household in anyway, yet he resided there also. Well, his clothes at least were there. He would buy me things *he* wanted me to have or give me money for a bill when *he* got ready!

I would not see Daniel Sr. for days at a time, and I would just pace my floors all night. I could not sleep, nor eat. I was just so broken inside. When he did emerge, he acted as if he had done nothing! I would question him about his whereabouts; he undoubtedly, would make up some outrageous lie and excuse. Consequently, my persistent interrogations would lead to verbal and constant physical altercations between he and I.

Nothing ever changed with Daniel Sr. He was just a dog! Women were always calling my home, hanging up, riding by my home, breaking Daniel Sr.'s car windows out, breaking my damn car windows out, and throwing eggs at my home!

I was so stupid and in love with a zero! I had given this low life ten years of my life, and cannot think of any happy times with him, ever!

After ten years with Daniel Sr., he finally left me for one of his tramps. I was 25 years old with a ten-year-old son, and my heart was broken. I felt like dying. He did not even have the decency to at least attempt a moral closure with me! Daniel Sr. was not even man enough to come and tell me that he was leaving. He just took one of his sabbaticals one weekend and never came back. I was heart-broken! He did finally re-surface about a month later to retrieve his clothes, of course with no remorse or explanation. He just cursed me out and went on to begin his new life!

I was really shocked to learn whom he had actually started see-ing. Leslie Potts was her name. She was one of the biggest tramps in the city and had a reputation of sleeping around with everyone's man. She was about 5'5," a chocolate complexion, which really surprised me, because I had always thought Daniel Sr. was in to "light skinned" woman.

Leslie was not bad looking. She had a nice shape; about a size seven or eight; however I've heard that she has ballooned up to 200 plus pounds! She had shoulder length black hair, and this unusu-ally large head. She also had big breasts which appeared to make her head wobble at times.

Leslie was much younger than Daniel Sr. He was 26 years old, and she was 18. She did not go to school, nor did she work, and lived at home with her family. I had heard the rumors about Daniel Sr. see-ing Leslie after the fact, and by that time, she was already pregnant with his child.

CHAPTER THREE

So there I was, a mess emotionally. Without a doubt, scarred for-ever. I could not even comprehend that Daniel Sr. was a human being! My heart was shattered! I felt so rejected, unloved, and un-wanted. There was no justified reason why I deserved this from him! I was faithful to Daniel Sr. and I loved him with everything I had!

I had taken so much from this man for so long, and this was how he repaid me! I always worked, paid my bills, took care of my son, and was certainly a lady. I was attractive enough, smart, and had much class, besides falling in love with him! I gave birth to his first son, his replica! Daniel Sr. was inhumane, and I will never forgive him for everything he had taken me through, and what he had done to me!

I was really embarrassed that Daniel Sr. had chose Leslie over me. I was hurt and humiliated, but I had to maintain for my son. My con-solation and strength was to know without a doubt that: *"Whatever a man sows, that he shall also reap,"* and Daniel Sr.'s reaping days were imminent!

I had not heard from Daniel Sr. until six months after his departure. There were so many rumors about him and Leslie flaunting around town and that Leslie looked like she would have her baby any day now. I was really broken inside, and did all I could to consume my mind and time. I was not seeing anyone, and had no intention, nor desire to affiliate myself with any man right now. I worked a lot of hours and was taking more classes at the community college. My son, Daniel Jr. spent a lot of time with my family and his friends. Dan-iel Sr. had made no attempt to contact Daniel Jr. or send me any monetary support for him.

One day Daniel Sr. called me out of the blue.

"What's up Raquel?"

"Not a thing Daniel," I replied, trying not to sound shocked to hear from him.

"Where is Daniel Jr?"

No, *"How are you Raquel? Do you need anything?"* Just to hear his voice triggers so many emotions for me, and I didn't like it!

"He is not here Daniel," I replied hastily hoping to get him off of the phone as quickly as possible.

"Where is he?"

"He is staying over with one of his friends," I replied.

"Oh, well I got some clothes for him, and I wanted to bring them by."

Daniel Sr. was a loser. He had not checked on Daniel Jr. at all since he left. Now he was calling, and wanted to play daddy. I had heard that Leslie had a baby girl. I guess some paternal inclination had kicked in.

I really did not want Daniel Sr. to come to my residence. I did not trust him, nor did I trust myself quite frankly. I did not know if it would give me some relief just to see his face again, or would it just send me into a rage. Neither prospect was good for me. But, I could not deprive Daniel Jr. of the essentials from his dad, and my son could use some new clothes.

Things had been a little tight for us. Daniel Jr. and I had moved to another location, and our moving expenditures were a little more than I had anticipated. But Daniel Jr. and I loved our new place, and I just wanted a fresh start away from all ties to Daniel Sr.

Daniel Jr. was involved in a lot of extracurricular activities, and he always needed money for something. As much as I hated to, I allowed Daniel Sr. to bring the clothes he had for Daniel Jr. I also had decided to ask him for some money for Daniel Jr. too.

"When did you want to come by Daniel?" I asked.

"I can come now," Daniel Sr. replied.

Now?

"Well, as I said Daniel Jr. is not home."

"I know, but I am in the area, and I want to come and get him this weekend anyway," Daniel Sr. said.

"I can just drop the clothes off for him."

"I will call later this week to set up a time to pick him up this weekend."

Oh, now he wanted to pick his son up and spend some time with him.

"Well, you know I have moved," I replied.

"Yeah, man, I know," Daniel Sr. replied to my astonishment.

"Do you know where we are now?" I asked.

"I know the town homes, but I don't know which one," he replied.

I can't believe him! This bastard had known that Daniel Jr. and I had moved all of this time. He never called to see if I needed any help, or did his son need anything! Daniel Sr. was just no good! He only cared about himself.

"Daniel, I am in Building 77." I could use a few dollars for Daniel Jr. too." I decided to slip that in, to see what he would say.

"Yeah, man, I will see," he replied.

Whatever! What is it that he had to see? He knew I could use some money from him to help me with Daniel Jr! I had already filed papers to put his ass on child support. I should have done it a long time ago. So, whether he likes it or not, his ass is going to help me with supporting our son!

CHAPTER FOUR

Daniel Jr. was eleven years old when his dad left. His dad did make some attempts to maintain a relationship with him, but Daniel Jr. was indeed affected by his dad and I tumultuous relationship. He loved his dad, but at the same time harbored a lot of resentment towards both his dad and me.

Daniel Jr. excelled in grade school, and we were extended the opportunity to allow him to skip a grade. I did not agree or allow Daniel Jr. to skip a grade, because he was always so much smaller in stature than his peers. I worried about him so much, even though he had a lot of heart, and was not afraid of anything or anyone.

When Daniel Jr. turned 14 years old, he had become so rebellious and defiant. Although he was very smart and even deemed "gifted," he began to get into minor trouble at school. He was getting detentions for skipping classes, talking, and incomplete assignments. He then progressed to suspensions. It was very difficult and caused a lot of heartache for me. Daniel Jr.'s behavior and attitude had really disappointed me.

By the time Daniel Jr. had reached high school, he had been to the juvenile detention center several times for smoking and selling marijuana. He was 15 years old at this time, and doing all kinds of things I would have never imagined him to do.

I had talked to Daniel Jr. vehemently about staying out of trouble and not ending up like his father. He thought he was grown, and neither I, nor anyone else could reason with him about anything! He was drinking, staying out all night, and doing all kinds of foolish stunts. I was so worried about him and afraid for him. I had been back and forth to court, writing letters, crying, and pleading with judges, counselors, everything to keep Daniel Jr. out of prison. I would have given anything for my son not to end up in jail, like his father. And God knows I did everything as best as I knew how to prevent that, to no avail.

Daniel Jr. did go through a lot of changes, and took me through a lot. He was just like his dad, unfortunately, in so many ways; selfish, disrespectful, manipulating, in and out of jail, and like his dad, did not give a damn about me. He only wanted what ever he could get from me, and I would give it to him if I had it. I think I was trying to compensate Daniel Jr. for whatever void his father had left by not being there for him.

I loved my son with all that was within me. As much as it hurt me to do so, I had to let go of my "baby boy." When Daniel Jr.'s turned 16 years old, his rebellious attitude and criminal activities resulted in him going to jail for two years. I was devastated, but it was nothing else I could do to protect him. He had made the choices he made and had to live with them. I finally "let go" and continued to pray that he would become the man that I knew he could and would. It was a lot of growing pains for him, and for me, but Daniel Jr. eventually got his act together and succeeded.

Daniel Jr. is now 24 years old, married, and has one son of his own. He adores his son, and is a great father. The paternal sustenance he provides into his son's life certainly surpasses his father's role in his.

He and his family live in Atlanta, Georgia now, and he is embracing a successful singing and music career. I was so very happy and proud of him.

My son did get his act together, and no accolades, go to his dad, but all to his *Father… Heavenly*, that is!

CHAPTER FIVE

Daniel Sr. arrived at my place shortly after I had spoken to him on the phone.

"What's going on Raquel?" Daniel Sr. asked with this silly smirk on his face.

"How are you Daniel?" I reply.

"I'm fine," Daniel Sr. replies. I extended my hands to o assist Daniel Sr. with a couple of bags he was holding.

Daniel Sr. looks good, and does not appear to have changed a bit since I last saw him.

"I hope I got Daniel Jr. the right sizes," Daniel Sr. says and helps himself to a seat on my sofa.

"I hope so too," I reply, glancing through the bags.

"The receipts are in the bags in case anything needs to be returned or replaced."

"Ok," I casually reply.

"So what's up with you Raquel?"

"You are looking good," Daniel Sr. says.

"Thanks." Daniel Sr. gazes around my home.

"You have a nice place here Raquel."

"Thanks."

"Daniel Jr. and I like it very much."

"So, who are you seeing?" Daniel Sr. asks.

I knew that was coming!

"What do you mean Daniel?"

"I know some guys have been hollering at you," Daniel Sr. replies sarcastically.

"Well, if I was seeing anyone, it's certainly no business of yours," I reply.

He has a lot of balls! How dare he question me about who the hell I am seeing!

"Yeah, you know better than that Raquel."

"You will always be my business."

"Daniel, I am not going to even respond to that notion," I reply.

"So, how is your new baby?"

"She is fine. She just cries a lot," Daniel Sr. stupidly replies.

That's what babies do, you idiot!

"So, when will Daniel Jr. be home?"

"How is he doing in school?"

"He is spending the night with a friend, and continues to do well in school," I reply.

"I miss my boy."

"Daniel, you were never here with him anyway!"

"Raquel, don't start that."

"No, you started it Daniel!"

The rage begins to stir in me. "You still have a son here!"

"He still needs a father too."

"You have been gone for six months and have not even called to check on him to see how he was doing!"

"Raquel, I have been really busy, but I will never just forget about my son's well-being," Daniel Sr. replies.

"You also need to be man enough to give me some money on a regular basis to help support him!"

"Raquel, I will get Daniel Jr. anything he needs."

"What about medical, dental, and his activities Daniel?"

"Just give me the bills, and I will pay them."

"Whatever Daniel!"

Daniel Sr. not giving me any money is just his way to try and maintain control over me! He just wants me to beg him, and I will not do that! I am not going to waste my time arguing with his ass about money for Daniel Jr.! I will see him in child support court!

"Hey, Raquel, I got something I need you to do if you want to make some money though," Daniel Sr. says.

"Really?" *I hope this scumbag does not think I am going to sleep with him!*

"Yeah, I need you to drive my car to Miami for me, and I follow."

"I will pay you a thousand dollars," Daniel Sr. continues.

Is this bastard soliciting me to do something illegal?

"Why do you need me to do that, Daniel?"

"And, you should just give me the damn money!"

"Man, Raquel, I don't trust anyone else to do it,"Daniel replies.

"Are you asking me to do something illegal Daniel?"

"Raquel, it's just a delivery I need to make, and you are going to make a thousand dollars!"

"Are you serious Daniel?"

"I cannot believe you have the audacity to come here, and ask me to do such a thing for you!!"

"You have got to be the worst of mankind!"

"It does not matter to you if I was to get caught, and go to prison, and my son is left with out a mother!" Daniel Sr. just sits there looking dumbfounded!

"Man, Raquel, nothing would have happened!"

"All you had to do was drive," Daniel Sr. says. *I don't know why I am so stunned with Daniel Sr.'s proposal to me. He was a selfish,* bastard, and did not give a damn about no one but himself! I was in tears now.

"Daniel, you will get everything that is coming to you!"

I did not even know what else to say to him!

"It is time for you to leave my home Daniel!"

"Raquel, you are tripping for nothing," Daniel Sr. says getting up to leave.

"I wish I'd never met you Daniel!" I yell to him as he makes his way to the door.

"You don't mean that Raquel," Daniel Sr. says sarcastically, and makes his exit.

I hate him! Daniel Sr. lacks all human decency! He was willing to jeopardize my life for his own selfish intents and desires! It did not matter to him that I was his son's mother, and anything could have happened to me! He did not care that if anything were to happen to me, Daniel Jr. would have been without a mother! I could have possibly even been killed! There were so many reasons for me to hate Daniel Sr. I desperately wanted to, and a part of me did! But, there was, just the same, a part of me that still loved him, and I don't know why!

A couple of months later, Daniel Sr. reaped what he sowed. He got caught trafficking cocaine, and was sentenced to prison for ten years.

CHAPTER SIX

Daniel Sr. had been in prison for six months before I received an unexpected call from him.

"This is the operator, and I have a collect call from a Daniel Blake," the operator said.

I know he does not have the nerve to call me! His ass got just what he deserved!

I started not to accept the call, but I thought about Daniel Jr. I had told him that his dad was in jail a couple of weeks ago. It was no need for me to keep it a secret from him because everyone was talking about it anyway.

"What is he in jail for?" Daniel Jr. asked.

"Drugs," I reply.

"This is why I tell you all of the time Daniel, to stay away from drugs and the wrong people!"

"You are too smart for that, and I do not want you to end up like your dad!"

"I know ma," Daniel Jr. replies.

"I am not crazy ma!"

"Yes, I will accept the call," I reply to the operator.

"Raquel?"

"Yes, Daniel."

"How you doing?" Daniel humbly asked.

"I am fine Daniel."

"Thank you for taking my call Raquel."

"Yeah, well I thought you might have wanted to talk to Daniel Jr., because it's no reason for you to be calling me!"

"Ok, Raquel, I don't need all of that from you."

"I did want to talk to my son."

"I wanted to talk to you too, but I see you are not up to that," Daniel Sr. says.

Damn Raquel! Don't start feeling sorry for his ass! He took no pity on you!

"Talk to me about what Daniel?" I reply.

"I just want to tell you that I am sorry Raquel," Daniel Sr. answers.

I was still harboring love for Daniel Sr. He was my first love: I just could not shake him, no matter how much I wanted to. I felt bad for him now. He sounded so alone now. So, I let my guard down and decided to give Daniel Sr. a little slack.

"So, what is going on with you Daniel?" I ask.

"Well, they gave me ten years, but I am hoping I can get out sooner for good behavior."

"Mmmmm, so are you ok?"

"Yeah, I am ok."

"I just hate to be in here."

"Well, I am praying for you Daniel."

"Thanks Raquel."

"Can I write you?" Daniel Sr. asks.

"Sure Daniel and I will write you back," I reply.

"Do you need anything," I ask.

"No, I am ok for now."

"I would appreciate if you would just write me, and send some pictures," Daniel Sr. says.

"I will see what I can do Daniel."

"Will it be ok for me to call from time to time?"

"Yes, Daniel, it's cool," I reply.

"Where is my son?"

"May I speak to him," Daniel Sr asks.

"Sure."

"Daniellllll," I yell to Daniel Jr. in his room. Daniel Jr. appears as if I had interrupted something he was doing.

"Daniel, your dad is on the phone, and wants to talk to you."

"I don't want to talk to him," Daniel Jr. replies heading back to his room at the same time.

Daniel Jr.'s response shocks me!

I follow Daniel Jr. back to his room with phone still in my hand, forgetting that Daniel Sr. is still on the phone, and can hear Daniel Jr. and I dialogue.

"What do you mean; you don't want to talk to your dad, Daniel?"

"I just don't want to talk to him," Daniel Jr. replies as he continues playing a video game.

"Daniel, this is your dad!"

"Come and talk with him now!" I demand.

"Maaa...I don't want to talk to him!" Daniel Jr. is crying at this point.

Daniel Jr. really had not said anything, or asked me anything about his dad since I had told him about Daniel Sr. being in jail. *I don't know if he was embarrassed or what.*

"Raquel, Raquel!" *Damn! I'd forgotten about Daniel Sr. being on the phone!*

"Yes, Daniel."

"Sorry about that," I continue.

"I heard my son, Raquel," Daniel Sr. says.

"He doesn't want to talk to me?"

"Don't make him."

"It's ok," Daniel Sr. says pitifully.

"I don't know what's wrong with him Daniel," I reply.

"I have to go now, but I will call him another time," Daniel Sr. says.

"Ok, I will talk with him Daniel."

"I am going to write you and Daniel Jr. a letter."

"Please make sure you write me back and send me some pictures."

"Ok," I reply.

"I love you Raquel."

"Love you too Daniel."

"Take care of yourself," I say.

"I will."

"Goodbye."

"Goodbye Daniel."

Daniel Sr. seemed so sad and defeated. I really felt bad for him. I still cared for him, and my heart was heavy for him, but he had brought this on himself. Now, he had to deal with someone else controlling his life for the next ten years probably! He was paying for all of his selfish, manipulative, ways, and everything he did to me!

Daniel Jr. was paying for his dad's absence too! I went in to check on Daniel Jr. after hanging up with his dad.

"Daniel Jr. you should not act like that with your dad."

"He needs you right now."

"You hurt his feelings not wanting to talk to him."

Daniel Jr. had resumed to his own time and thing, playing his video games.

"Ma, I just did not feel like talking with him."

"Are you angry with him Daniel?" I ask.

"No, he does not do anything for me," Daniel Jr. replies to my amazement.

"Daniel, he is still your dad, and he loves you."

"When he calls you again, I want you to talk to him, ok?"

"Ok, ma," Daniel Jr. replies, and I exit Daniel Jr.'s room.

Daniel Sr. continued to call from time to time, so that he could talk with Daniel Jr. Daniel Jr. never wanted to talk to him. I would have to make him talk to his dad. Sometimes he would adamantly refuse to talk with him. I think it made Daniel Sr. feel bad.

I would try to explain to Daniel Sr. that he had to understand what Daniel Jr. was going through.

"He has a lot of resentment towards the both of us."

"We took him through a lot with our relationship," I would tell Daniel Sr.

"He felt abandoned by you when you left his life and started another family," I had told Daniel Sr.

"Daniel Jr. is my first son, and I love him very much," Daniel Sr. would proclaim.

"I know I was not there with him as I should have been, but I love my son and did all I knew how."

Daniel Jr. resented his father, and that was something he and his father had to work through. I never tried to dissuade him from having a relationship with his father. In fact, I would encourage him to, but he simply wanted nothing to do with him.

CHAPTER SEVEN

Daniel Sr. had been in prison for a year now. He would call from time to time, and we would write each other occasionally. Even though he had treated me like crap, I did not have it in my heart to disengage. Leslie, his girlfriend was running around with all kinds of guys and had spent all of his money, Daniel Sr. would tell me. *Well you got what you wanted Mr. Blake!*

"I was a fool to leave you Raquel," Daniel Sr. would say. He needed a friend right now, and I was at least trying to be that to him.

I eventually started "casually" dating again; however, none of the relationships were really significant for me. I was still in love with Daniel Sr. but I had resolved to the fact that we would never reconcile. My tolerance barometer had decreased considerably. So, I was just not taking any nonsense from anyone! I wanted what I wanted in a man! I wanted a genuine partner in every aspect, and was not cutting any slack. If I was not getting all that I wanted in the relationship, then there would be no need to continue, and I did not.

Then there was Clyde. I'd never thought that I could fall for another man as I did for Daniel Sr. until I met Clyde. Clyde was so fine; smooth, mocha skin, alluring bronze eyes, a grade "A" body, pretty teeth, and appeared to have *capable* lips. Clyde owned and operated one of the most popular barbershops in the city.

Everyone knew Clyde, and the ladies were crazy about him. I had met Clyde at his barbershop. Daniel Jr. went there for his weekly ritual haircuts. He was very particular about his haircuts, and favored Tim, whom was one of Clyde's barbers and close friend.

Tim was not available to cut Daniel Jr.'s hair one day, but Clyde was. Clyde extended his services to Daniel Jr., and to my amazement, Daniel Jr. agreed.

I think Daniel Jr. was impressed with Clyde's charismatic approach. He later told me that he thought Clyde was really cool.

I was looking pretty good. I'd lost a little weight and was wearing it well! I always kept myself pretty much together, and was not into "keeping up with the Jones." I retained my own style and finesse, and I was comfortable with it. That was all that mattered to me. Clyde was indeed checking me out! Some mutual acquaintances of Clyde and I had told me, that he had made inquiries about me before. I had also heard that he had a girlfriend, but he was **not** married!

On some occasions when I would drop Daniel Jr. off to get his hair cut; Clyde would not charge him. Daniel Jr. would come home and tell me that Clyde asked him if I had a boyfriend. I knew Clyde liked me. He had a woman, and I was not trying to hurt anyone or break up anyone's home. I knew better than anyone that pain, and certainly did not want to impose that on anyone else!

I had no intention of getting emotionally involved with Clyde, but he was so charming and magnetic. Of course, I knew, as with most men, that is a part of their bait. I had not been with a man in almost a year, and I was lonely. I was open to some sexual healing, passion, and relief! I wanted the comfort of a man. No commitments, just some companionship right now.

One day when I took Daniel Jr. to Clyde's shop for his weekly haircut, Clyde was there. Daniel Jr. now only wanted Clyde to cut his hair. Clyde had several other patrons waiting for him, but he summoned Daniel Jr. to his barber chair.

Clyde's alluring eyes truly mesmerized me as they pierced mine. As he looked into my eyes, I felt as though he was looking in my soul, and quite frankly, that thought frightened me and enticed me the same.

"Have a seat, pretty lady," Clyde said to me as his eyes embraced me from head to toe. "I will take care of Daniel Jr. for you. It will only be a few minutes. "Can you wait for him?" Clyde asked me in a persuasive tone.

"Sure, I can wait," I replied.

"Do you want anything to drink or eat? Clyde asked thoughtfully. "No, I'm fine, thanks!" I reply.

Clyde proceeded to cut Daniel Jr.'s hair, taking his time, very methodically, and with such passion. He was very   neat and professional, encouraging Daniel Jr. to alert him how he wanted his haircut. He also frequently made inquiries about any special style or features he wanted. As I watched Clyde, trying my best to appear engrossed in my magazine, my imagination got the best of me. One eye was sporadically reading my magazine, and the other eye, along with all of my other sensual senses, were piercing Clyde as he mastered his gift of cutting my son's hair.

My thoughts immersed in a trance as I began to imagine Clyde and I making love. I wondered if his loving was as passionate, meticulous, and cautious as his art of cutting hair. Did he take his time? Would he encourage me to tell him just the way I wanted it?

I noticed Clyde's eye's piercing me as well, on occasion. He was checking me out, but I pretended not to notice. Clyde seemed like he was a confident, daring man, and that was so attractive to me.

He made no pretense of his alluring stares at me. When I would pretend to take a repast from my magazine, Clyde's eyes would meet mine with such an engaging smile. I welcomed his gaze, returning a sheepish smile that was undoubtedly in agreement with his thoughts. At least I had hoped.

Clyde finally finished Daniel Jr.'s haircut, and my baby looked as handsome as always. Daniel Jr. admired himself in the mirror as I walked over to Clyde to pay him.

As I proceeded to give Clyde my twenty-dollar bill, he extended his hand to retrieve it, and said to me softly, "Can I walk you outside? I need to talk to you."

Talk to me? That response alarmed me. What on earth did Clyde have to talk to me about? I hoped Daniel Jr. had not said or done anything.

"Ah, sure," I hesitantly replied.

Daniel Jr. had finally retreated from admiration of himself in the mirror.

"Are you straight, my man?" Clyde asked Daniel, Jr.

"For sure," Daniel Jr. responded, smiling and adoring himself again in the mirror.

"Thanks Clyde," he said pleasingly.

"Are you ready, Daniel?" I asked.

"Yes, Mom."

Daniel Jr. and I head to the door, and Clyde followed.

"I'll be right back," Clyde assures one of his patrons.

I could feel the entire barbershops' eyes follow us to the door. Daniel Jr. grabbed my car keys and headed to the passenger side of my car, allowing Clyde, and I some privacy. I was nervous to hear what Clyde wanted to say to me and anxious at the same time.

CHAPTER EIGHT

Clyde led me to the rear of my car, and I followed him feeling a little apprehensive. He leaned confidently with his arms crossed aligned his chest, and against my car. I faced him to give him my full attention, and my body tingled in expectation of what Clyde had to say to me.

"Raquel, you know you are a beautiful woman," Clyde said to me assuredly.

"Thanks," I replied.

"You know I'm feeling you a lot, and I'd like to see you, take you to dinner, whatever you want to do, but most of all, I want to get to know you personally."

Just like that, Clyde said what was on his mind. I stood there pretending to be so surprised. *What in the hell do I say back to him?*

"Really," I replied sarcastically.

"Really," Clyde responded before I could say anything else. "I know a lot of guys are at you, but I think you and I are destined to get to know each other better."

"I've been checking you out for a long time."

"I confess I have even made some inquiries about you."

"I've had dreams about you at night, and I think of you all day." Clyde smiled seemingly to redeem himself from revealing his nocturnal thoughts of me.

Clyde's recital line, "I dream about you at night and think of you all day" seemed authentic to me. Maybe, subconsciously I just wanted it to be. "I am flattered, Clyde."

Clyde retracted from leaning against the car and walked toward me. He gently grabbed my hand and began to caress it. *What do I do now? What the hell do I say?* I am really intrigued with Clyde, but I do not want any problems. Clyde is so sexy, and I would like to get to know him better.

"So Clyde, what about your woman?" I asked incisively.

"Well, I can't be anything else but honest with you, Raquel."

"I'd certainly hope so, Clyde."

"I do have a lady, Raquel." Clyde says as a matter of factly.

"I just need a chance to talk with you and hopefully get to know you better," Clyde said with a hint of desperation in his voice. This alarmed and intrigued me at the same time.

"I am not trying to play you Raquel, or take advantage of you."

"Just, let me take you to dinner and we can talk some more. Then you can ask me anything you want about my situation and decide from there," he concluded.

I pondered Clyde's invitation as he continued to penetrate my eyes magically. *Why not? What wrong with dinner?* I was very attracted to Clyde, and wanted to get to know him, as well. I was not trying to break up anyone's happy home or hurt another woman. I truly am not that kind of person. I really like Clyde. How could I turn down a proposal that I had desired so much? *Just do it, Raquel,* I convinced myself; although I think my mind was made up when Clyde posed the invitation.

Clyde interrupts my thoughts. "Here is my number, Raquel," Clyde said. "Just have dinner with me," Clyde reiterates.

As I extend my hand to retrieve the number from Clyde, he gently massages my hand and kisses it with those insatiable lips. I thought I was going to melt, but I maintained my composure, at least for the most part. Our eyes met with anticipation and expectation.

"I'll think about it, Clyde," I said, knowing full well I most definitely would be in touch.

"You will not regret it," Clyde responded with a confident, skirmish grin. He began to retreat back inside the barbershop, but not before bidding Daniel, Jr. goodbye. I noticed something transcend from Clyde's hand to Daniel Jr.'s. I remained standing in one place, somewhat in a trance, as I watched Clyde glide to the entrance of the barbershop. As Clyde's hand reached for the door, he turned back to catch me still standing where he'd left me. I was in awe of what had just happened. Clyde was beaming with an engaging smile and yelled, "Raquel, so I can expect a call from you tonight?" Clyde asked assertively.

"Perhaps," I responded, attempting to sound half interested.

Clyde paused for a moment, piercing my eyes with his intoxicating bronze eyes and seductive, smile. I was in a trance, and literally could not move. He then turned and retreated back to his clientele. I finally gained my composure and came back to earth.

CHAPTER NINE

Was this really happening to me? Daniel Jr. intrudes my thoughts with his persistent yelling.

"Momma, come on. I got to get my things to go to Wade's house."

Wade was Daniel Jr.'s God-brother. He and Wade were inseparable. I made my way to the driver's seat of my car, still in a bit of a trance. In route back to my car, Daniel Jr. must have noticed my transient state of mind, and decided to assist me by having my car keys in the ignition. As I shifted my gears into drive, my thoughts were on nothing but Clyde. I was really flattered with Clyde's interest in me, and it made me smile inside.

"Momma, Clyde gave me fifty dollars." Daniel Jr. says beaming with excitement.

"Oh yeah," I replied. *Damn, fifty dollars!* "What did he give you fifty dollars for?"

"Momma, I know he likes you, and I like him, too."

"Yes, I guess you do," I replied sarcastically. "So he just gave you the money for nothing?"

"Yup. He told me to take my girlfriend to the movies," Daniel Jr. replied.

Daniel Jr. was growing up. He was turning 13 years old in a few months. I could not believe it. Daniel Jr. was always small in stature for his age, but he had a huge, confident attitude. He was extremely charismatic and loved by everyone. Daniel Jr. was into girls now, and they were into him. They would call my home everyday, constantly for Daniel Jr. I was always yelling at him about that. Every chance I got; I talked to Daniel Jr. about sex. He seemed to be receptive, and I just prayed to God that he would come to talk to me before he engaged.

"Oh yeah? That was real cool, huh?" I replied to Daniel Jr.

"Yeah, Clyde is real cool mama. You should go out with him," Daniel Jr. continued, which really confirmed my intention to call Clyde.

Daniel Jr. didn't like any man with his mother but his father. I think he really wanted me to be with his father, but resented Daniel Sr. for the way he had treated me. I hated that my son had to go through that, and I would never allow such drama into his life again. It really affected Daniel Jr. He trusted no man with his mother, but I could tell he admired Clyde. I was happy about that, because momma liked him too!

I'd like to think that I am a decent woman, with decent values. I was not in the business of taking another woman's man, but Clyde really intrigued me. I was so attracted to him, and not just physically, but I enjoyed his ability to really communicate with a woman, while also allowing her to respond.

I was also lonely. It had been over a year, and I had not been in any serious relationship since Daniel Sr. Daniel Sr. was like this worm that invaded and infiltrated my mind, body, and soul, a disease that I wanted it.

I decided that I would give Clyde a call when I got home. Ultimately, I knew deep down inside I was going to do what I wanted to do. And the truth of the matter was that I really would like to get to know Clyde. Was the risk worth it with Clyde? I didn't know, but I had already made up my mind to take that chance.

CHAPTER TEN

Jill Scott once said, "It does not matter who you are loving, just as long as you are loving." I concur.

Daniel Jr. and I finally made it home from Clyde's Barbershop. Daniel Jr. was excited about the extra spending money he had received from Clyde. His weekend excursion plans with Wade became more appealing to him. I was engrossed with thoughts of Clyde, and looking forward to a private, unrestrained conversation, and perhaps meeting with him.

Daniel Jr. hurriedly gathered his gear to go and spend the weekend with Wade. I was tidying up a bit, preparing for my meditation time alone, and looking forward to calling Clyde. Daniel Jr. burst into my room, where I was cleaning up, to tell me that I did not have to take him to Wade's house, because he and his mother Janine were coming to pick him up. That was a relief for me and would allow me more time to myself so that I could process my thoughts.

"Daniel, I want you home Sunday evening, no later than 9:00 PM. Make sure you take you toothbrush and deodorant," I reminded him.

"Momma, I got them. Okay, Momma," Daniel Jr. replied tirelessly.

I did not mind Daniel Jr. spending time at Wade's home. Wade's mother, Janine, and I were good friends, and she was Daniel Jr.'s godmother. Her family always treated Daniel Jr. like part of their family. Janine loved Daniel Jr. as if he were her son as well, so I was always comfortable with him spending time with them. Wade was a good boy, and had such a cool demeanor. He was my favorite out of all Daniel Jr.'s friends. Wade and Daniel Jr. were like brothers. Wade was the only one who could keep Daniel Jr. in line, for the most part.

Janine and Wade arrived about an hour later to pick Daniel Jr. up. It was Friday, and Daniel Jr. was not returning home until Sunday. I had the entire weekend for Raquel and whatever I wanted to do. I don't know why, but I was in the mood to go out!

CHAPTER ELEVEN

Daniel Jr. was gone for the weekend, and I decided to go out for some socializing. I was still thinking about Clyde, but I was not quite ready to give him a call yet. Even though, I really wanted to call Clyde and get to know him better, I also had a lot of reservations. I knew that Clyde had a girlfriend, and that certainly posed a big problem for me. I did not want to become entangled in any love triangle, and any heartache or drama for no parties.

I took a shower, got dressed, and headed out for a night on the town. Maybe me going out would take my mind off of Clyde.

I arrived at the club and the place was packed with people. I was looking good and a lot of guys were checking me out. As I made my way to a vacant spot at the bar to get me a drink, I noticed a couple of women at the end of the bar staring at me in a contemptuous manner.

It was Leslie, Daniel Sr.'s girlfriend along with a couple of her ghetto girlfriends. I almost did not recognize her; she had ballooned up to 200 plus pounds! I could not believe it! *Damn!* Daniel Sr. had been in prison for a little over a year now. There were all kinds of rumors about all the men Leslie was messing with, and how she had ran through the little drug money he had left. She must have done a lot of eating out too!

There had been some tension between Leslie and me under the circumstances, but I had left all that alone and went on with my life. She had always been so jealous and insecure about me, when I posed no threat to her at all!

Daniel Sr. would call me sometimes and tell me all kinds of lies Leslie would tell him. She had told him that I was calling her, and riding by her house, where as, I knew of no telephone or address for her! Even, if I did, why would I stalk her? It was a ridiculous notion. I was not angry with her. Daniel Sr. chose her. I was beyond Leslie and Daniel Sr.'s nonsense. I knew Daniel Sr. would always instigate much of the tension between Leslie and me because that made him feel "big" about himself.

I had a feeling there was going to be trouble. I had too much of a good time at the club, and Leslie, along with her "posse" had been watching me the entire night.

As I proceeded to leave the club, Leslie and one of her girlfriends accosted me in the parking lot. Leslie was talking all of this smack, showing off in front of her girlfriend.

I had seen Leslie alone at times right after Daniel Sr. went to prison, and she'd never confronted me in any way. She knew not to, because I would kick her ass!

Leslie continued to mouth off with me, and I was trying to avoid any confrontations and just go home. I really did not want any trouble and certainly did not want to mess up my outfit. But before I knew it, I had slapped Leslie so hard in the face my hand was tingling! The fight was on, and I was defending myself with both Leslie and her girlfriend! I was furious! Some people finally broke up the fight, and Leslie and her girlfriend took off running like the cowards they were!

CHAPTER TWELVE

Some guys at the club walked me to my car to ensure that I was ok. I was fine, except for a ripped blouse. I was so pissed! *Leslie better not let me catch her by herself! Her ass is mine! She would have never tried me like that if she was alone!* I thought about calling Rachel, but decided against that because Rachel would have wanted to go look for Leslie and her posse. I did not want Rachel or myself to get in any trouble and go to jail. I could not wait until I heard from Daniel Sr. tired ass! I knew Leslie was going to tell him all kinds of lies and make like I was the culprit. I really did not give a damn what Daniel Sr. thought or believed. He and Leslie both were very disturbed and immature!

I finally made it home from the club. *I cannot believe these tramps jumped me!* I don't even know who Leslie girlfriend was, but I had seen her with Leslie before. I will find out when I talk to Daniel Sr. again! Her ass was mine too!

A myriad of thoughts filled my head as I proceeded upstairs to take a warm bath. Should I call the police on Leslie? No! I will get her ass myself. Leslie is just a fat, jealous, insecure tramp! She knew she was not in my league! That's why she hated me so much. I'd never done anything to her. She was so afraid that Daniel Sr. and I were going to reconcile. I still was in love with Daniel Sr. but I had no desire to reconcile with him. And me loving him would pass too someday. All it took was another.

As I began to undress, my mind became consumed with Clyde. It was 12:00 midnight, and I wondered what Clyde was doing. I really wanted to talk to him now. I did not even know if he and his girlfriend were living together. He never mentioned that to me. Why would he have given me his number to call if he was living with someone?

I grabbed my bathrobe and headed to the bathroom to take a bath. The warm water was very soothing to my body. Damn; I'd wish I had poured me a glass of brandy before immersing in this water. Resting my head on my bath pillow, I closed my eyes for some much needed meditation.

CHAPTER THIRTEEN

"Raquel?"

"Hi Rachel."

"Are you ok Raquel?"

Damn! Rachel had heard about the fight I had with Leslie last night! I can hear it in Rachel's voice!

"So what's this I hear about Leslie and some chick jumping you at the club last night?" Rachel asks angrily.

"Who told you about it Rachel?"

"You know how people talk Raquel!"

"I just heard about it today!"

"Why didn't you call me?"

"They said you beat both of them though," Rachel laughs.

"I am ok Rachel."

"I was out last night at Sparkles, and they both confronted me as I was preparing to leave."

"You should not go out by yourself anyway Raquel," Rachel scolds.

"You know how jealous hearted those women are!"

"Who was the chick with Leslie fat ass?" Rachel asks.

"I don't know, but I have seen her with Leslie before."

"Did they hurt you or scratch your face or anything?"

"No, thank God Rachel."

"They only tore my blouse and some guys broke it up."

"Everyone is talking about it Raquel."

"They said you slapped Leslie so hard, they thought her head would fall off," Rachel said laughing fiercely.

"Really?" I was laughing now thinking about the ordeal myself!

"She (Leslie) better not let me see her anywhere," Rachel says.

"Rachel, I don't want you getting into any trouble!"

"That's why I did not call you."

"Did you call the police Raquel?"

"No, I did not, Rachel!"

"I did not want all of that drama."

"You better hope Selena and Sashe do not hear about it," Rachel says. Selena and Sashe were my two younger sisters.

"I hope not, and please do not tell them Rachel," I plead.

"Where is my nephew (Daniel Jr.)?"

"He is at Wade's house for the weekend."

"OK."

"Give me a call later on Raquel," Rachel says.

"I will, and thanks Rachel."

"For what?"

"Loving my big sis," Rachel says and hangs up.

Glad that interrogation is over! I should have known that Rachel would hear about the fight. I'd just hope it did not get back to my other siblings. I was fine, and it was over, and I just wanted to move pass it! I was still very angry about it, but I wanted to carry on.

It was Saturday, and Daniel Jr, was not due home until tomorrow. I still had one entire day to myself, but I wanted to check on Daniel Jr. It seemed as though he was at Wade's home more than he was at home. Janine, Wade's mother would always insist that I allow him to stay, because Daniel Jr. loved being over there.

I was going to spend the rest of the day relaxing, and rejuvenating at home, alone. Maybe, I will give Clyde a call today.

I made me a nice hot cup of tea and lit a cigarette. The first drag of my cigarette relieved me momentarily from all of the tension I was feeling. I sat down on my sofa to watch some television, and begin flipping through the channels. Nothing was of interest to me on television, so I popped in a movie from my massive collection. It felt good to just stretch out on my sofa and do nothing. I'd hope Daniel Sr. calls me today so I can tell him off about his ghetto ass woman! I'd expected him to call me with some nonsense and lies Leslie had told him about the fight. I was ready for him too, and would have no more pity on him and his sad songs! He and Leslie both were losers and deserved each other!

I really was not even watching the movie I had put in. I was thinking about so many things. Clyde probably was at work right now and really busy. *Raquel, just go ahead and give him a call. You are not going to be satisfied until you do! Oh what the hell!*

"Hello."

"Hi Clyde."

"Yes, may I help you?" *Damn! He did not even recognize my voice! I felt like hanging up.*

"Clyde, this is Raquel," I finally say.

"Raquel?"

"Heyyy pretty lady," Clyde says "How are you lady?" Clyde asks.

"Are you busy?" I ask.

"Not for you," Clyde replies.

"What's up with you?" Clyde asks. Clyde never called my name. I got the impression he did not want to let out who he was talking with.

"Are you ok?" he asks.

I sure hope he had not heard about the incident last night. I certainly did not want him to get the wrong impression of me. I am not a bar brawler, but was simply defending myself.

"Yes, I am cool."

"Why do you ask?"

"Mmmm you sound a little tense," Clyde says chuckling.

"Oh, well I am a little," I stupidly reply.

"Do you have any plans this evening?"

Oh my goodness…what do I say?

"Uh, not really."

"Okkk, let's get together for dinner," Clyde affirms.

"Dinner?"

"Yes."

"I will pick you up at 7," Clyde says.

"Ok, but you don't even know where I live," I reply, not knowing what else to say.

"Be ready at seven."

"I will call you when I am en route for directions," Clyde says.

"Cool?" Clyde says.

"Cool. I will see you then," I conclude.

CHAPTER FOURTEEN

Clyde and I begin a roller coaster affair. When Daniel Sr. left me, my self-esteem, and confidence left me as well. I had lost hope in loving again, or someone ever genuinely loving me. Clyde re-invigorated me, and it felt good! He was so easy to talk to and that is what made me fall for him initially. Clyde was soothing to my broken heart, and I needed that! I wanted that!

A month after "secret" dinners and various entertainments, we made love for the first time. Clyde was a passionate lover, which was important to me. I appreciated his passion, because I was too; therefore, our lovemaking was extremely satisfying to us both.

I knew that Clyde was in a relationship when we begin our affair. Clyde was even honest with me about them living together. I had anticipated and expected Clyde to make a decision about Chloe and I, and we argued constantly about it.

I knew Chloe. I did not know her personally, but I knew of her from mutual acquaintances that she and I had. Chloe was an attractive, educated, classy lady. She had come from a very good family, and her daddy gave her anything she wanted. She knew of me as well, but I don't think she knew of Clyde and I affair. I don't even think that she was aware that Clyde was having an affair at all.

Clyde and I had been seeing each other for about a year when I was crushed with a startling confession he had made to me. He and Chloe were engaged to be married! They were engaged six months ago, and wedding plans were in preparation for next year!

"Married!" I yelled.

"Why in the hell didn't you tell me this Clyde?" I asked.

"So you asked her to marry you even after you and I began this?"

"What the hell was **this** Clyde?"

"Us?" I asked.

"She wants to get married, but I don't. She has always been there for me." Clyde replied.

"You cannot love two people, Clyde," I had told him.

"Yes, you can, Raquel," Clyde would respond frustrated and upset.

"I know that you are still in love with Daniel Sr.," Clyde would yell back at me.

I know damn well he is not trying this reverse psychology on me!
"Dammit, Clyde, that is not fair!"

"No, but it's true, Raquel, and you know it. Do you think I am crazy? Whenever he calls, you talk to him. And your conversation is not always about Daniel Jr! I've even heard that you have been writing him and have been to see him," Clyde confessed angrily.

"He sent word by some people to let me know! It kills me inside to know that you still allow him to manipulate you."

I was crying at that point.

"I could not really confront you about it because of my situation, but I *am* in love with you Raquel," Clyde said adamantly. I was so ashamed and crying fiercely at this point. Clyde was right. As much as Clyde meant to me, I was also still harboring some feelings for Daniel Sr. I didn't understand it all myself.

I could not shake Daniel Sr. It was *something* still there for him. I can't explain it! *It* just would not go away! I had been to see him a few times in prison. I had also taken Daniel Jr. to see him. I still cared for Daniel Sr. but I had no intention of reconciling with him!

Clyde did help me somewhat with the restoration of my self-worth and esteem, but I had a long way to go. Ultimately, I knew only I could fix things within myself. No one was capable of actually doing it for me.

"Yeah, that's what I thought," Clyde answered the question himself. "Raquel, you want me to be with you solely, but you can't let go of Daniel's ass."

"Do you think I am going to accept that?" Clyde angrily asked. *How dare he ask me such a question!*

"What about me, Clyde? Do you think that I am going to continue to tolerate your lame ass excuses and you marrying her?" I responded.

"Raquel," Clyde said exhaustingly.

"We need some time apart," I said.

"Okay, you are right," Clyde said. "I need to make a decision, and you need to make a decision. We cannot continue going through this. At least I was honest with you from the beginning; I never lied to you about anything."

"So what, Clyde, you think that makes it all better for me? I want a life, a real life, my life, my man, and my future! Can you give me that?"

Clyde paced the floor in anguish.

"Yeah, that's what I thought," I concluded.

Clyde turned and stared at me pitifully. "I don't want to lose you, Raquel, but I need some time."

My eyes pierced his, and I could literally see his anguish, but hell, I was hurting too! I walked to the door and opened it for Clyde to exit.

"You take all of the time you need, Clyde."

Clyde glared at me trying with all of his masculinity not to show any emotion or a tear, and slowly walked towards the door. As he proceeded to make his exit, he turned to look at me. I could see the water in his eyes, and he gently kissed me on my neck and whispered in my ear, "I do love you." He then turned and walked away.

I asked myself, what is my excuse for falling in love with someone else's man? Another man who cannot or will not commit to you solely? Why are you so broken, so damn needy, so vulnerable, so giving that you feel like you have to tolerate this crap? You are worthy of so much more from a man, your own damn man for starters.

The finality of Clyde and I last conversation hurt me so much. Deep down inside of me, I knew he was right about he and I having to make a decision about our relationship. I did love Clyde, but I had to face the fact that we had no imminent plans for a future. And that is what I wanted, a future! Clyde knew that!

CHAPTER FIFTEEN

As much as I had loved Clyde and wanted a chance at a real relationship with him, his engagement to Chloe was it for me! I had resolved that it was time for me to move on, and get my act together. I was tired of this! It was quite obvious Clyde did not love *me* enough to dissolve his relationship with Chloe to allow us a chance. He would always tell me how unhappy he was within their relationship. He told me that he loved her, and respected the woman that she was. Clyde said that Chloe had put of with so much from him and stood by his side. He also confided in me that he was just not stimulated sexually and passionately in their relationship.

I broke it off with Clyde after his revelation to me about him and Chloe's engagement. Clyde called me constantly for several weeks.

"I know you do not understand this, Raquel, but you make me feel like no woman has ever made me feel, even Chloe."

"Raquel, please do not take this the wrong way."

"I love your passion."

"Your love is amazing to me!"

"I am truly in awe, and you have so much love to give."

"You make me feel something I have never felt before."

"You are so compassionate and sensual."

"I am not just talking sex Raquel." "I love everything about you."

"I can **feel** your love when we make love, and I just don't want to lose that feeling ever!"

"It completes me in a sense."

"Raquel, you complete me!"

I continued to listen to Clyde intensely.

"And her?"

"What do you love about her?" I asked hesitantly.

"I love you, Raquel, but I love her, too. I know that is difficult for you to understand."

"I love her strength, her loyalty, and her putting up with me," Clyde responded.

"Oh, and I have not done that for the past year, Clyde?"

"Yes Raquel, you have, but I have to go on with this wedding. Raquel, she is counting on me."

I glared into nowhere for seemingly an hour. I could feel my eyes watering and tears began to trickle down my face. *Hell, I am count ing on you, too, Clyde. What about me? If he felt all of these things for me, why isn't he and I walking down the aisle? I had to be real with myself, because I already knew the answer. He is full of crap, just like the rest of the guys!*

But I still and always will, love him. This is what I get for stooping to this level and allowing myself to be the "other woman", but Clyde was so persistent! That was my excuse for falling for him, which really did not matter at this point. The fact was that I fell, and frankly, I just did not know how I was going to recover from this one! I just could not believe he had done this to me!

Clyde was such a smooth operator, I'm convinced he had Chloe in check, just the way he wanted her. Who the hell was I kidding? Clyde had wooed me just the same. I guess my part in his egotistical mind was the sexual, passionate void in his relationship with Chloe.

Daniel Sr. had heard about Clyde and I relationship. He had been calling me with his taunts and threats. "Raquel, how the hell are you messing with a man that already has a woman?" Daniel Sr. would taunt me. "You might as well have dealt with me." I would never have given Daniel Sr. the satisfaction, and let him know how right he was! It was a difficult time for me, and I was so afraid of crumbling again.

I loved Clyde, and I missed him terribly. A couple of months after Clyde and I break up, I succumbed to his pleas to see me and "talk" and our affair resumed. We continued an "off and on" affair for the next eight months. I would break it off with Clyde, but somehow we would always find ourselves back together again.

CHAPTER SIXTEEN

I was not feeling well and had taken the day off from work when the phone rang.

"Hello, Ms. West," a man's voice emerged.

"Yes, this is she."

"This is Sergeant Adams of the Tampa Police Department, and we have your son, Daniel, in custody for possession of marijuana."

Damn, Daniel Jr., here we go again! "What?" I yelled.

"He was caught on the school grounds at Courtney High School with two pounds of marijuana in his possession."

"What?" I yelled again.

"Calm down, Ms. West," the officer uttered, seemingly sympathetically. "I know Daniel. Unfortunately, I arrested him before, and I know that you are upset. He is going to be transported to the Juvenile Detention Center and will probably see the judge tomorrow."

"Oh my God," I began to sob.

"Ms. West, as I stated earlier, I have dealt with Daniel before. I know that you are a good, caring mother. I have talked to you before about Daniel. This is the reason that I am giving you this information on his transport. Normally, we do not have to disclose that."

"Thank you, Sergeant Adams. I appreciate that very much. Is he going to have to do any time?" I asked.

"Quite frankly, Ms. West, I am pretty sure he is going to have to do the twenty-one days in juvenile. He needs to learn a lesson."

"Twenty-one days? Oh my God! What about school?" I began to cry again.

"Ms. West, Daniel made his own bad choices, and you cannot save him. I can understand your support of him, and I commend you for that, but Daniel needs to take control of his own life and future. You will not be able to accomplish that, only he can do that," Sergeant Adams counseled me.

"I know, Sergeant Adams. Thank you. When will I be able to see him?"

"You can see him tomorrow in court at 9:00 AM, sharp."

"Thanks again, Sergeant."

"You are welcome, Ms. West, and Daniel is okay. Please try and get some sleep tonight," Sergeant Adams implored.

"Thank you, Sergeant," I repeated.

"Goodbye, Ms. West."

My God, I don't believe Daniel Jr.! *"God, please help my child,"* I prayed. *"Please take care of my child, your child."* I then I began to cry uncontrollably for seemingly hours.

CHAPTER SEVENTEEN

I finally dragged myself out of bed and made my way to the kitchen. I was feeling even more defeated now after the news about Daniel Jr. I turned on the coffee maker to make myself a cup of coffee. The aroma of the coffee stimulated me a little, but my mind was still consumed with Daniel Jr. I poured myself a cup of coffee and lit a cigarette. Boy, it felt good as I took a cautious sip of my coffee and a nice drag from my cigarette.

Lord, please give my baby another chance. Don't let them keep my son, and please take care of him and keep him safe.

I don't know what I would do if something happened to Daniel Jr. He was all I had, and he was the reason I remained on this earth. If it were not for him, I would have "flown" away a long time ago. I loved my son more than anything. I wish he knew and understood that, and it would somehow compel him to do better with his life.

Although he resembled, and acted so much like his father; he was *not* his father! I knew somewhere in him was me...his momma, some goodness, compassion, and love.

Daniel Sr. had called me, and I told him about Daniel Jr. I knew I had not done everything right in raising Daniel Jr., but Daniel Sr. certainly was at fault too!

Daniel Sr. would never accept responsibility for Daniel, Jr.'s defiance. Of course, he blamed me for everything that was going on with Daniel Jr.! Daniel Sr. thought that as long as he acknowledged Daniel Jr. as his son, and bought things for him, that was enough to justify him as a father to Daniel Jr.! He would not admit or face the reality of how he had failed Daniel Jr. He was never there for Daniel Jr. as a father should be. He never spent time with him, as he should have, whether he was in or out of jail.

Recently, Daniel Jr. and I relationship had become so combative. He was 14 years old now. He just thought he was grown and could do what he wanted to do. I would get on him about staying out so late at night, and he was getting into trouble in school.

Also the fact that I had him so young, we sort of grew up together. The tumultuous relationship his dad and I had, definitely scarred him too. Daniel Sr. was never around to help raise him. He was always running around with tramps or in jail. I did the best I could to raise my son, but certainly made some grave mistakes.

One major thing is that I did not discipline him like I should have, so I spoiled him and allowed him to get away with so much. I had no parents to confide in, or run to for solace. I never knew my father. And my mother, as much as I have always loved her, offered no maternal guidance, ever. She had her own issues.

I never really knew how to be a mother, because I was never mothered to. My siblings and I had raised ourselves, and each other. So I made a lot of mistakes raising Daniel Jr., but I never, ever, neglected him! He always had a roof over his head and food to eat. I was always there for him, but I *spared the rod*, and I paid for that dearly.

CHAPTER EIGHTEEN

Daniel Jr. did his 21 days in the juvenile detention center and was then allowed to come home. I had been to see him about five times while he was there. I was so angry and disappointed with him and he knew it! I had asked him where in the hell did he get marijuana from? Of course, he was adamant about "it not being his," and he was "holding it" for a friend! I knew he was lying, and would never tell me the truth about it.

"Daniel, you will be turning 16 years old very soon. You will not be going to the juvenile courts again if you continue to do your own thing! You will be going to the adult system! That is adult prison and years," I had told Daniel Jr. He was responsible for his choices just as everyone else, and would have to live by them. He promised me he would do better.

Thank God, Daniel Jr. was allowed to return to school. I had made several calls and wrote letters to the School Board pleading for him to be able to continue his education. A few of the officers at the juvenile facility had also sent letters of recommendation on Daniel Jr.'s behalf too, at my request. The School Board approved Daniel Jr.'s re-admission to school. They felt that he could reform. I was so grateful for their decision in allowing Daniel Jr. a second chance.

Daniel Jr. had always exceeded in academics and athletics with little effort. He was a star football athlete, and had received numerous academic and athletic awards. Daniel Jr. also had already been offered several academic scholarships. He was well liked by his teachers, and coach.

Daniel Jr. was the first African-American Freshman Prince named at his high school for homecoming; an honor that made me so proud of him. I had a lot of dreams for my son, and I'd hope that he was going to be someone great, and make me proud of him.

CHAPTER NINETEEN

I could not believe the "big" day had finally arrived. Tomorrow Clyde and Chloe were getting married! I was a mess! Clyde and I were still seeing each other. I felt like Clyde was the only man I could really love after Daniel Sr.

Clyde and I had spent a romantic evening together. It was awesome and very passionate. I wondered how he could be with me like that when he was getting married the following day.

We talked about so many things, our relationship, and *his* relationship with Chloe, as well the impending "Grand Wedding." Her parents had spent a lot of money on the wedding, and he *had* to marry her. We also talked about "the baby." Yes, on top of everything else, I was now carrying Clyde's baby.

Clyde had pleaded with me for months to have his baby. He promised me that he would be there for our child and me always, no matter what. Clyde had two beautiful daughters from a previous relationship. He adored them, and he was really a great father to them. They lived in another state, but Clyde would get them every summer and they would spend the entire summer with him and Chloe. Chloe did not have any children, but Clyde told me that she wanted to have children. He confided in me that he thought that she might be having a problem conceiving. They had been trying to no avail.

Clyde would tell me that he wanted me to have his child because our child would be a part of me, and how much he loved me.

"You are a beautiful woman, Raquel, inside and out," Clyde would endear me.

"Yes, but what about my child's future and my future as well, Clyde? You know I would love to have your baby, but I want to be married."

"Raquel, I would never desert you or our child. I will always be here for you."

"Clyde, you are marrying another woman and getting ready to embrace a whole new life with someone else," I would tell him.

"I know, Raquel, and we've been down this road numerous times. That does not deplete what you and I have, and you know that."

I really loved Clyde's profession of his claim to love and cherish me so much. I believe that he did, but just did not know how to break it off with Chloe. At least that was the excuse I told myself.

Clyde constantly pressured me about having his child. I knew it was just his way of keeping me in his life. What in the hell was I going to do with another child right now with all of the turmoil going on in my life? I really could not afford one. Clyde and my relationship surely had me frustrated all of the time. Daniel Jr. was driving me crazy with his defiant attitude, and getting in and out of trouble. I just did not think I was ready for such an impact in my life.

But because I loved Clyde and had hoped that we would have a future together someday; I gave in and became pregnant with his child. Clyde was elated when I told him. I was happy and so fearful at the same time.

Daniel Jr. had been giving me so many problems, and he certainly is not going to be happy about this. Although he did like Clyde, I'd thought he would be a little jealous. Surprisingly, when I told Daniel Jr. the news, he seemed happy about it.

"Really? I always wanted a brother or sister," Daniel Jr. replied to my amazement.

"Are you happy about the baby?"

"Sure, Mom, but you know my daddy is going to have a fit."

"I don't know why, he is making babies all over the U.S., so he claims," I replied defiantly.

"Yeah, but Momma, you know he is not going to like that; especially you and Clyde. He hates Clyde."

"Well, that's *his* problem. He is just mad I am continuing on with my life, and he no longer has any control over me."

"Yeah, but you still love my daddy, Momma, and you know it," Daniel Jr. concluded and headed for the door.

I was relieved when Daniel Jr. exited so that I did not have to respond to his conclusion of me still loving his dad. As much as I hated to admit it, he was right.

I had not heard from Daniel Sr. in a couple of months. I don't think he knew about my pregnancy because he surely would have something to say. I was only a couple of months, and no one really knew but Rachel. Of course, she was disappointed in my decision to have this baby. But it was my choice, and despite of everything that was going wrong in my life, I was now happy about this baby.

CHAPTER TWENTY

We were in my bedroom listening to music, and Clyde's head rested in my lap while I stroked it lovingly. Clyde embraced my stomach gently and kissed it with such sincere affection. I could tell that Clyde was going to love our baby very much. We were listening to *Anita Baker*, whom Clyde loved, and listened to her for hours. Clyde and I both said nothing. Clyde seemed oblivious to all.

We were both very emotional the entire week leading up to the wedding. We argued. We cried. And we made passionate love. There was nothing else to be said. It was what it was, and we both had to deal with it all. Somehow, someway, especially with me, decisions had to be made. Clyde was getting married tomorrow.

Clyde intruded my thoughts as he began to console me. While kissing me passionately, he told me that everything was going to be all right. We made passionate love again, for seemingly hours.

Afterward, I watched Clyde as he showered and got dressed. He seemed a little distressed, perhaps, and exhausted after our marathon love making. Clyde grabbed his keys off of the dresser and waltzed over to me while I was still lying in bed exhausted myself; yet still feeling and desiring him.

He kissed me gently on my forehead, and whispered in my ear, "I love you."

"I love you too," I said. Clyde smiled confidently and exited out the door.

That was the last time Clyde and I were together.

CHAPTER TWENTY ONE

It was Clyde's wedding day, and I was a mess! Ironically, I had another wedding I was attending today for two of my co-workers. I had committed to going and I would make it there with God's strength.

The wedding I was attending was at 2:00 PM, and Clyde's wedding commenced at 4:00 PM. It was already 10:00 AM, so I really had to get moving and pull myself together.

I had always dreamed of myself walking down the aisle one day. No matter what was going on in my life, I still had faith that it would happen someday.

I felt so drained, and had such an uneasy feeling as I made my way to the shower hoping to rejuvenate myself. Of course, I was really depressed about Clyde's wedding today, but I was feeling more than just heartache. It was an eerie feeling that something was going to happen today, and it was not going to be good.

Something was desperately wrong. I just did not know what, but I felt so damn eerie this morning. I woke up with so much frustration and anxiety. It felt like a dark shadow was hovering over my head. I could not understand why I had such a strange, melancholic attitude and perception this morning.

It was Clyde's wedding day, and he was not marrying me. *That must be it!* That is why I felt so gloomy and discontent.

I had spent my last evening with Clyde last night, and it was so painful seeing him leave to run off to marry another woman.

Rachel had called to check on me, well actually lecture me!

"Damn, Raquel! Why do you keep taking yourself through this crap? You have no one to blame but yourself!"

"And I don't blame anyone but myself!" I try to explain to Rachel.

"You really need to get some backbone girl!"

"You do not deserve this shit! You can do better! You are not a bad looking woman; you are intelligent, articulate, loving, self-sufficient, and independent, with so many hopes and dreams! Why do you settle for so much less than you are truly worthy of? You do not have to take the crap that you do! You are a good woman, and you do deserve to be respected and honored for the woman you are. You cannot continue to keep giving to these no good ass men, and not receive the same from them! You cannot continue to fall for their crap! And you have to love and respect yourself, and no matter what, believe that you are certainly worthy, because you are! Ok, SO, you are so broken, that's your damn excuse! Well, fix it damn it! Fix it! Fix all of this turmoil that you have succumbed to! So, are you going to continue to mourn over how you allowed Daniel Sr. to treat you, and everything he has done to deplete you, and hurt you? You know you should have left him way before he had left you! He was never any good to you, or for you!"

"And Clyde was never any good for you either! Why? Because he had a WOMAN! And once again, you allowed yourself to be the OTHER WOMAN! You allowed Daniel Sr. to rob you of your self-respect, and your self worth! When are you going to get it together girl? Fix it girl! Not next week, not tomorrow, but today! Fix yourself Raquel! So now you think you love Clyde? And maybe you do, but whom in the hell loves Raquel? You do, don't you? Don't you love yourself, or at least want to love yourself? Then fix it Raquel! You are going to have to pick yourself up, and shake all the shit off! That's right, shake this shit off! Haven't you been through enough, taken enough? You put up with Daniel Sr. and his shit! And now Clyde! Sure you and Clyde have had some good times together, and he has never mistreated you, and has done some nice things for you and with you, and he may even care about you somewhat, but HE IS MARRYING ANOTHER WOMAN TODAY Raquel!"

Rachel had given me an entire "re-cap" of my life, and I did not like it!

"So where does that leave you?" Rachel finally asks me a question, but does not allow me to respond. "That's right, still alone, and probably even more broken than you were before you met him! Fix it Raquel, and please for God's sake…. carry on!!!" Rachel concluded and slams the phone.

My body started to tremble. Rachel was right about everything. Somehow I made it back to my bed, trying to fight what was coming next, but it was inevitable. As I retreated back to my bed, the tears were already prevalent. I lied in bed immersed in tears and cried myself sick for two hours, continuously telling myself to, "Fix it, Raquel."

CHAPTER TWENTY TWO

Clyde had left a frantic phone message. His tone was surely that of frustration. He was talking about having to see me tonight, and he would think of something to tell Chloe.

Now, I was feeling somewhat sorry for Clyde. That was my damn problem; always considering someone else's feelings and well being and neglecting my own.

I began to pray as I headed to the shower.

"Lord, please take care of Daniel Jr., me, and this baby. Please keep us safe and covered in the Blood of Jesus. In Jesus name, I pray, Amen." As I proceeded to my shower, the phone rang which startled the hell out of me.

"Raquel?"

"Clyde?"

Oh my God! It's Clyde, calling to tell me that he can't go through with the wedding!

"Hey baby," Clyde said.

"Hey Clyde," I responded, beaming with my hopeful thoughts.

"I wanted to call and check on you to make sure that you were okay."

"I'm okay," I lied. "How are you, Clyde? So you will be a married man in a couple of hours?"

"Yes," Clyde replied hesitantly.

" Hmmmm," was all I could get out.

"Raquel, I love you, and I hope you know this will not change things between us," Clyde said nervously. What the hell does he mean? Of course it is going to change things between us. What the hell am I supposed to do henceforth? I wanted to get married someday, too, and share my life with someone. And since Clyde was marrying another woman today, it was apparent that it would not be him.

"Clyde, what am I supposed to say?" I asked exhaustingly.

"Baby, please just be there tonight," Clyde pleaded. "I need to see you tonight."

"What do you mean; you need to see me tonight?" I asked Clyde, somewhat shocked with his demand. "It's your wedding night, Clyde. Not that I am supporting it, but the bride and groom are supposed to be together on their wedding night," I replied sarcastically. "I know you told me that you and Chloe were not taking any honeymoon because of this "Fairy Tale" wedding Chloe had planned, but how are you going to get away to see me tonight, Clyde?"

I was really shocked that he even suggested such a thing. Of course, I would love to see Clyde tonight and every night for that matter, but I had really convinced myself that once Clyde said "I do" to Chloe, then I was going to say "I don't" to him.

"Clyde," I finally calmed down to comfort him. "What is the matter, Clyde? You seem so uptight. Are you having second thoughts, or are you just nervous or something?"

"Raquel, I can't lose you, baby."

Okay, now I was really concerned about Clyde. He really sounded desperate.

"Just be there tonight, okay, Raquel? I'll call you when I am on my way over, okay, baby?"

"Okay, Clyde," I calmly replied to ease some of the tense energy I was receiving from him. "Clyde," I continued hesitantly. "You know you do not have to go through with this wedding if you are not ready. Not just for my sake, but for your sake as well, especially if you are not ready for this commitment."

"I have to go through with it, Raquel. Chloe is counting on me. You and I have talked about this, right?"

"Right," I gave in.

"I have to go, Raquel; I'll call you tonight."

Clyde hung up the phone, just like that! I never would have imagined it would have been my last time talking to him.

CHAPTER TWENTY THREE

I was still holding onto the phone, a bit in shock after Clyde had hang up. That creepy feeling returned to me again. I finally regained my composure and hang up the phone. As I glanced over to the digital alarm clock on my dresser, big red numbers displayed 12:35PM. I took a warm shower and proceeded to get dressed for Lance and Lacy's wedding.

I had promised my co-workers Lance and Lacy that I would be at their wedding today. I damn sure was not in the mood, but they were counting on me.

Lance and Lacy were the cutest couple! I was very happy for the both of them; although, I had wished it was I walking down the aisle with Clyde. I began to get sad and angry at the same time. I was sad because I was lonely, and I was angry at Clyde! I wanted someone special to share the rest of my life with. I knew I would be a good wife. I was a good, faithful woman, but just seemed to always attract losers. What the hell was the matter with me? Who in the hell does Clyde think he is? Does he think I am just going to sit around and continue to be the other woman? I loved his ass, but I wanted to get married and settle down, too.

It was 1:15 PM, and the wedding starts at 2:00 PM *Okay, Raquel, you looking good*, I told myself as I check myself out in the mirror. I really did not look too bad. I was two months pregnant with Clyde's baby, but I was not really showing I had put on a beautiful sapphire Liz Claiborne silk dress that Clyde had bought me when he went to visit some family in New York a couple of months ago. He really did have good taste.

"Baby, I saw this and I knew it was you," Clyde had explained to me when he presented me with the dress. "I know you like glitter and glamour, and I thought you would look beautiful in it," Clyde continued. The dress fit me like a glove. He really knew me pretty well, which sometimes amazed me.

Clyde would always tell me he liked my style and the way I carried myself.

"You are a classy lady, Raquel, but what intrigues me so much about you is that you still maintain a sense of humility at the same time. That really turns me on," Clyde would lovingly appeal to me.

"Thanks Clyde," I would reply, loving his compliments as always.

I've got to get my ass out of here now. I checked myself once more before I departed for Lance and Lacy's wedding. I wish Clyde could see me in this beautiful dress he'd bought me. *Forget Clyde; his ass is off getting married his damn self!* I am so angry and hurt at the same time, yet I could not help but think about. It should have been me marrying Clyde today. But Clyde made his decision, and I had made mine, too! I am cutting his ass off and out of my life! As Clyde embarks on a new life, I am going to do the same!

Damn, it's one-thirty! I grabbed my keys and headed to the door. As I hurriedly approached my car, I could feel someone watching me. It was my next-door neighbor, Cedric. Cedric was a real sweet guy, about five years my junior, and I knew he had a crush on me. Unfortunately, he was married with three children. His wife, Kate, was about ten years his senior. She was a nice lady, and I was quite fond of her. I think she had an inclination that her husband had a little crush on me, but she never really let on her thoughts to me. I never gave her any reason to think that anything was, or ever would be, happening between Cedric and me.

Kate was not a bad looking woman herself for her age. She was forty-six and could easily pass for ten years younger. She kept herself up, looking good, worked everyday and certainly appeared to be a good mother and wife from what I could see. She would come over and talk with me sometimes, and it was always good things about her husband and how much she loved him. He was a good man and father. That was evident to me.

Cedric was good looking, had a nice body and the sweetest personality. One thing for sure, Kate was very lucky to have him, and quite frankly, I think he was fortunate to have her as well. They really made a nice couple. I never knew them to argue, or any nonsense to go on in their household. They seemed to be the perfect family, which I envied at times. Their kids were also respectful, and cordial.

Asia, their youngest daughter really got attached to me, and I her. She was six years old. A beautiful little girl with long curly hair and a smile that would make one melt indeed.

I loved my son with all I had, but I'd always wanted to have a little girl as well, so I pretended like Asia was my daughter, and she loved that. She always came knocking on my door to show me her dolls, or what she did in school that day. I would always have treats for her and buy her things at the store, so she really loved me for that. Her parents did allow Asia to visit me. They knew how much we adored each other, and I would take care of her like she was my own. Asia had spent the night with me sometimes, after much pleading with her parents and me. We would bake cookies together and paint each other's nails. I had bought her a pretend makeup set, after checking with her parents, of course. Asia and I would then make up each other's face. Asia really enjoyed that.

"Hi, Cedric." I waved as I got in my car.

"Hi, Raquel, you look stunning," Cedric replied.

"Thanks, Cedric, I am off to a wedding."

"Well looks like you may be prettier than the bride," Cedric replied flirtatiously.

Cedric worked hard for his family, and took good care of them. If his ass were not married, he would surely be a good catch for me. I pretended to not hear Cedric's last response. "Kiss my girl, Asia, for me," I yelled to Cedric and started my engine to make my way out of the driveway.

CHAPTER TWENTY FOUR

I really had to push it. It was 1:35 PM, and the wedding was to start in twenty-five minutes! My mind and heart both were racing at the same time, not to mention me racing to get to the wedding.

Traffic always seemed worse when I was trying to get somewhere in a hurry. I couldn't help but to think of Clyde. I loved his ass, but I had to end this shit tonight. He seemed adamant about coming over after his freaking wedding. I was angry, but I did want some closure. I want to do it right, face-to-face with Clyde. I knew he was going to do everything in his power to convince me not to leave him, and may even threaten me about this baby, but I had made up my mind. I could not continue this relationship with Clyde; I simply could not handle it anymore. Now I am having his baby. I knew I was going to have to deal with him on that aspect, and I would, as civilly as I could, but I am serious about getting on with my life. I want this baby, too, but I will not have Clyde. It ends today, and I mean that!

I wanted Clyde to be a part of this baby's life, and I know he will. He will do well by this child. His ass certainly better, because he knows I will make sure that this baby is taken care of by *Clyde*. I am settling for nothing less in that respect. Clyde wanted this baby and promised me he would be there for it, and he damn sure better be.

Wow! The church was packed. As I walked into the church, I began to feel a little faint. *Damn, Raquel! Don't start this crap now! Keep it together, girl!* I waved nervously to a few co-workers and headed straight to the bathroom. I made my way to the sink and splashed a little cold water on my face, trying desperately to keep it together and not distort my make up. I didn't know if it was the baby that's giving me the jitters, or just walking inside a church attending a wedding on the same day Clyde was to be married! *Oh my god! Clyde will be getting married himself in a few hours! Lord, please help me keep it together.*

I got that eerie feeling again; a bad feeling like something was going to happen.

Oh God, please don't let me lose this baby. I don't know what's going on with me. I felt fine when I left home, well as fine as I could.

"Raquel, are you okay?" a voice asked behind me as I was bending over the sink grasping for air. It was Siara, one of the girls I worked with. I managed to hold my head up.

"Hi, Siara," I replied nervously.

"Can I get you some water or something?" Siara asked.

"Yes, thanks," I said.

Siara hurried out of the bathroom and returned momentarily with a cup of water for me to drink. I drank the water, which helped a lot, and tried my best to regain my composure.

"Are you going to be okay? The wedding is getting ready to start."

"Yes, I am fine, just a little faint."

"Why don't you come sit with me?" Siara asked.

"Thanks, Siara; I appreciate that." Siara handed me a napkin to wipe my face. She and I then headed to the sanctuary.

I had not revealed to anyone that I was pregnant yet, except for Daniel Jr., Rachel, and Siara. Siara was a sweet, modest, Christian woman, who was well liked and respected by everyone at work. She was about thirty-five to forty years old, slim figure, reasonably attractive, and divorced with two children. She was very friendly and always supporting and encouraging people at work who appeared to be down or having a rough time. It was not her being nosey or invasive, but she had a genuine, humble, and empathetic approach that brought me a lot of comfort many times.

Siara was my confidante' at work. She was the only one I had confided in at work *about* my pregnancy, and my affair with Clyde. I was not ready to make any official announcement on my job about my pregnancy, and my baby's daddy was no one's business. I was fully aware of some of the invidious women that I worked with who *did* know of Clyde and I affair. That could not be helped, due to the small city we lived in, so the rumors were rampant. I really did not give a damn what any of them thought, because a lot of their situations were worst than mine.

I had not even talked with my boss yet. Siara was easy to talk to. She never tried to pry into anyone's business, or lay any guilt trip. Siara would always tell me, "Raquel, be of good cheer. Jesus has overcome the world, and so shall you."

CHAPTER TWENTY FIVE

The church was beautifully decorated, all in blue and white. Everyone had been seated, and the wedding was beginning. The bridesmaids wore beautiful baby blue satin gowns, and the groomsmen wore white tuxedos with blue satin shirts. They all looked quite stunning. As they graced us with their immaculate entrance, right behind them followed two of the cutest flower girls I had ever seen. One was in a blue satin chiffon dress, and the other girl had on a white identical dress. I imagined both girls to be about seven or eight years of age. The one that appeared to be the youngest reminded me of my neighbor's daughter Asia. Both girls were so cute. Closely following them was the ring bearer. He was adorable. He reminded me of Daniel Jr. about ten years ago, so he had to be about four or five years old. He exhibited no fear and held his plateau out with the ring on it like a true champ. Everyone in the church was beaming.

Just as the "little man" made his way to the rest of the wedding entourage, the traditional wedding music began, and everyone gasped as the star of the show appeared with her father's arm tucked tightly in hers.

Lacy looked beautiful. She wore a traditional, modest, cream-colored satin, long-sleeved wedding gown, along with the tiara, and veil slightly obscuring her natural teardrop, which undoubtedly had to be tears of joy and happiness. Lacy was marrying her soul mate. She and Lance were perpetual. Why else would she shed a tear? Everything was beautifully done. The church décor, her wedding party, flower girls, and ring bearer all were flawless!

Her father, who appeared to be about fifty, was quite distinguished, just on appearance itself. He was about six foot two, really handsome, nicely built and proportioned, well-groomed mustache, and low cut hair that displayed a natural grain of matured gray hair, which suited him perfectly. You could see that Lacy was indeed his "little girl," and that he was a proud father as he walked his daughter down the aisle cautiously, securing her arm, and checking on his "little girl's appearance with every step they made.

I began to cry, undoubtedly with a myriad of thoughts. Lacy was so fortunate. Hell, I did not even know where the hell my daddy was; I hardly knew anything about him. I thought about how beautiful Lacy looked and how happy Lance looked as he watched his bride make it down the aisle into his arms.

Here I am, carrying the man I am in love with baby, and his ass is marrying someone else today as well! That should have been Clyde and I...*there I go with that again!* I was happy for Lance and Lacy, but certainly envious at the same time. I could not help it. My life was so messed up.

To my relief, Lance and Lacy's nuptials were over. The reception was immediately after, and I had to attend, at least for a little while to give them my well wishes and the beautiful silver-plated, engraved wedding frame I had got for them as a gift.

I just wanted to make it to the reception. My plan was to stay for about an hour and then head home. I was still feeling a little light headed and really wanted to get home to my bed.

Clyde's wedding was the only thing on my mind. I glanced at my watch and it was 3:35 PM That meant Clyde and Chloe would be saying *their* "I do's" in about twenty-five minutes. Damn it! I felt like running. *Where in the hell was I going to run?* I didn't know. I really felt like running to the church where Clyde and Chloe were about to be married and demand that Clyde not proceed with the wedding. And if he did, I meant it this time. We were done and he would not have any part of our baby's life.

But, I knew I could not do that. I've embarrassed myself enough allowing myself to get caught up in this mess, falling in love with Clyde, and now having his baby. Not that this baby is an embarrassment. I wanted this baby just as much as Clyde did. I was afraid of having to raise another child on my own, and quite frankly, I really could not afford to.

As the wedding party exited the church, the guests followed close behind with cheers and warm regards. Everyone was en route to the reception that was taking place at Lance and Lacy's church hall. The church hall was directly across the street from the church, which I was glad about not having to travel any further, until I was ready to head home. As I exited the church, I was alarmed with someone tapping me on my shoulder. I turned around to see that it was Siara summoning me.

"Hi, Siara."

"Hey, Raquel, are you feeling a little better?"

"Yes, and thanks for getting the water for me. I just felt a little dizzy."

"Sure, Raquel," Siara responded, genuinely concerned. "The wedding was beautiful, huh, Raquel?"

"Yes, it was," I replied. "Lance and Lacy looked so happy."

My mind began to ponder on my unhappiness and disappointment with Clyde.

"Are you heading to the reception?" Siara asked. "I was hoping you and I could sit together. I came by myself, and you didn't come with anyone; did you, Raquel?"

"No, sure Siara; we can sit together, but I am not going to stay long," I replied.

"I think I need to get home to get some much needed rest."

Siara gazed at me with a sense of sympathy, like she could actually see my broken heart. But she dared not pry. "Okay, let's go, Raquel so we can get a good seat," Siara replied convincingly. Siara and I headed over to the church hall for Lance and Lacy's reception.

CHAPTER TWENTY SIX

Everyone else from the wedding was en route as well. We made our way through the crowd somehow and managed to get a good table right in front of the wedding party's table. Everything was beautifully set up. The tables were immaculately adorned with blue and white silk table cloths, a beautiful 5 X 7 engagement photo of Lance and Lacy displayed in a white ceramic frame shaped like a dove was their centerpiece on each guest table. *What a clever idea*. Also the tables were draped with fresh white and red rose pedals. *Now that was very romantic*. Each table had white china aligned with flawless stainless steel utensils. Also, red cloth napkins shaped like roses were firmly affixed in the middle of each dinner plate. It was simply breathtaking, I thought.

The décor in the church hall was nicely done; all of it complementing each other, and the ambiance of the room illuminated the tables' décor. The wedding party's table was adorned with a red silk table cloth, soft azure china, and crisp white cloth napkins shaped like a rose affixed firmly in each participant's dinner plate. *Very creative*. Lacy's parents had to have spent some money on this!

I began to think about Clyde's wedding. I wondered what the ambiance was there. I visualized Clyde all debonair in his tuxedo walking down the aisle with Chloe. I began to feel sick again in my stomach. Thank God, the wedding party made their grand entrance. That deterred my thought process, and I tried my best to camouflage my pain by smiling, attempting to obscure my impending tears. *Lord, please help me get through this reception,* I pleaded at heart.

Most of the guests were seated already, and the wedding party finally took their places at their assigned table. Servers were making their way to the tables to pour champagne in preparation for the guests and wedding party to simultaneously toast the newlyweds. I knew I should not be drinking any alcohol because of the baby, but the way I was feeling, I did not think one glass of champagne would warrant any harm, so I opted to partake. I needed to calm my nerves and relax a bit.

After everyone was served the champagne, the best man, Keith, whom was Lance's best friend since junior high school, appealed to everyone for his or her undivided attention.

I had met Keith before. He was really a fine brother, *but* he was married with two children. He was a narcotics detective. His wife, Linda, was one of Lacy's bridesmaids. Linda was a cute, petite woman. She was a nurse. I thought she and Keith had the picture perfect marriage, until Keith had hit on me.

I was out one evening at a club, alone. Keith was there and approached me at the bar where I was sitting. "Hi, you are Raquel, aren't you?"

"Yes, I am, and just how do you know me?" I ask.

"I don't know you, but have seen you around. I know your son's father Daniel Sr.," Keith replied.

Well, that made some sense, because most people knew of me from Daniel Sr., and our tumultuous ten-year relationship. Not to mention Daniel Sr.'s notorious reputation of his womanizing scandals.

"In fact, I have arrested him a few times," Keith says seemingly proud.

"Oh, well in that case, let me buy you a drink," I reply.

"No, Raquel, the pleasure would be mine to buy you one."

"Sure," I said.

"So you are a cop?"

"Actually, I am a narcotics detective," Keith confidently replied.

"Interesting," I replied.

"And so are you, Raquel," Keith responds.

"Well, I will take that as a compliment, Mr. Keith."

"It is, by all means."

"You are an attractive woman, Raquel," Keith continued to serenade me.

"Thank you."

Keith summoned the bartender. "Please give the lady whatever she wants," he told the bartender. "I will have a shot of scotch."

"Ma'am, what would you like?" the bartender asked me.

"I'd like a glass of brandy on the rocks," I replied.

"Coming right up," the bartender says.

"Thank you," I replied. Then I turned to face Keith and thanked him, too.

"Anytime." Keith smiled. "So, what's wrong with your man allowing you to come out alone?" Keith asked.

"What's up with your lady to allow you to come out alone?"

"I asked you first," he laughed.

I took a sip of my brandy, which rushed straight through my body. I could feel Keith's eyes undressing me, and I welcomed his imaginative thoughts, but he was married. He gave it away when I inquired about "a lady," and he did not rebuttal! Not to mention the fact of the wedding band on his left finger! I certainly was not going to take this trip. Been there, done that, and currently doing that, in dealing with Clyde's impending marriage. *Hell, that's why I was out alone.* The man that I was in love with was getting married in a couple of months and probably at home lying up with his future wife.

"Aren't you married?" I blurted out to Keith. Keith took a cautious sip of his scotch, and hesitantly responded, "Yes, I am married, Raquel."

"So, why are you in my face?" The brandy and I both reply.

"Because I think you are very attractive, and you intrigue me. For the record, I'd like a chance to get to know you."

"Keith, I am not into married men."

"I understand that, and I certainly do respect that. You should also know that I have never cheated on my wife, but I would love to take you to dinner and talk," Keith replied with sincerity.

My mind and body were racing simultaneously. Keith was so fine. I took another precautionary sip of my brandy, undoubtedly to soothe my mind and muster up enough strength to tell Keith to beat it. The temptation to embrace Keith's advances towards me was unbearable.

"Excuse me; could you bring the lovely lady another glass of brandy?" Keith instructed the bartender.

I considered the possibility that he was trying to get me drunk, but I was in control. I would love to meet another man to get my mind, body, and soul off of Clyde. Keith would have been a sure prospect. He was fine, intelligent, charming, smelled so damn good, professional, but married. I did not need to lead this man on any further. I could not regress to the same situation I was already in with Clyde. It was so frustrating and draining.

My thoughts were interrupted with the bartender alerting me to a freshly prepared glass of brandy he'd adorned just for me, compliments again from Keith. I responded with a nod of acknowledgment and gratitude.

"So how about breakfast, Raquel?" Keith asked graciously.

I needed to wrap this up, because I knew if I had breakfast with this man, it's definitely on!

"Keith, I do appreciate your courtesy, and for whatever it is worth, I am attracted to you. The fact of the matter is that I am currently seeing someone, and I do not under *any* circumstances relate with married men," I conclude.

I did it! Damn, that was hard. Keith glared at me with this innovative smile, and again, cautiously sipped his glass of scotch.

"You are a class act, Raquel," Keith said.

Not knowing if Keith was being sarcastic or genuine, I defensively said, "I will take that as a compliment, Keith."

"Oh, by all means, Raquel, it was certainly a genuine compliment."

Keith summoned the bartender. *Is he ordering more drinks for himself? It couldn't be for me, not after I just gave him the boot.* Keith pulled out his wallet and handed the bartender a hundred dollar bill. "Make sure the lady gets whatever she wants, and if needed, make sure she is escorted home safely via taxi," Keith ordered the bartender.

"Yes, sir, Mr. Chase," the bartender replied.

No, he didn't. Damn, Keith! Now that really impressed me! I did not know what to say at that point. I wanted to tell Keith, *"Sure, let's have an affair,"* but I knew better than that. Instead I said, "Keith, thank you again for your generosity, but you did not have to do that."

Keith took the last sip of his drink and pulled a card out of the left top pocket. He leaned towards me and kissed me on my cheek, while handing me the card at the same time.

"Please call me, Raquel, if you change your mind."

He then turned and exited the lounge.

CHAPTER TWENTY SEVEN

Lance and Lacy's reception was really nice and everyone seemed to be enjoying themselves... partying, drinking, and dancing. The food was good, and the music was great. I could tell that Lacy's parents spared no expense because there was plenty of everything. I danced a few times with a couple of the groomsmen, and I was beginning to have a little fun, until I got this slight pain in my stomach. It was not unbearable, so I continued dancing with Rich, whom was Lance's younger brother.

Rich was pretty handsome, and appeared to be about 25 years old. He was about six feet, with naturally wavy hair, and piercing emerald eyes. Rich was attending medical school in Washington, D. C. Lance had told me, at one time, that his "little brother" had a crush on me. I thought nothing of it, until now.

Rich had repeatedly come over to the table where Siara and I were sitting to ask me to dance. I declined until the fourth time he came over and told me that he would sit there at my table all night until I gave him one dance.

"Well, Rich, you will be sitting by yourself, because I am going to be leaving momentarily," I replied, slightly irritated with Rich's encroach.

Siara had excused herself a few minutes prior to go socialize with some of the guests, so I was left there alone.

After having no choice, Rich and I evolved into some conversation, which turned out to be quite gratifying to me, and eventually I welcomed his company. Rich talked about his educational pursuit and career plans and even shared with me a little of his relationship plights. We had talked a little during the course of the reception, and he told me that he had a girlfriend in DC, but they were not serious. According to Rich, the only thing he could commit to right now were his studies. He was quite articulate and intriguing; definitely more mature than his age.

"Raquel, you know I always had a crush on you," Rich said.

"Oh really," I replied surprisingly.

"Yes, I used to ask Lance about you all of the time."

I reached for my glass of cranberry juice that I downgraded to, and slowly took a sip of it, while thinking about how to respond to Rich.

"I am flattered, Rich" was all I could muster. Rich's eyes penetrated mine for a few seconds, which triggered spots of sweat down my back!

"So, Raquel, I hear that you are dating Clyde," Rich inquired abruptly, and leaned back in his chair as if he was awaiting an explanation from me.

"Oh yeah? Where did you hear that from, Rich?" I asked.

"Everyone knows it, except, of course, his fiancée, or she may be his wife by now," Rich concluded with a glance to his watch, and a bit of a smirk, which really set me off.

"Rich, I really do not care what everyone thinks or knows, and I do not care to discuss **my** business with you or anyone else because that's precisely what it is, my business," I replied emphatically.

"Okay, Okay, Raquel," Rich responded. He then leaned forward towards me and embraced my hand gently, as if to say, "I am sorry." Instead he said, "I just think you are a beautiful woman, and I would like just one dance with you. Forgive me, Raquel, I certainly did not mean to upset you." He then affectionately kissed my hand.

Well, that did it for me! "Fine, Rich, let's dance," I surrendered.

Rich escorted me to the dance floor, which was full with everyone dancing to *R.Kelly's Step* song. Rich then embraced me with *his* "step dance" version, and I slowly but surely began to groove with him. He was really a great dancer, and all eyes were on us. I began to get in the groove with Rich. We really made a good pair. Rich seemed to really be enjoying dancing with me, and I damn sure was having fun with him. We danced a few more times, which proved to be too much on the baby and me.

Without any warning, I got a sharp pain in my stomach, which halted our dance flow. Rich noticed the intense pain in my face and grabbed me, just as I thought I was about to faint.

"Raquel, are you okay?" Rich asked.

"I just need to sit down for a minute, Rich," I nervously replied.

Rich practically carried me off of the dance floor. The dance floor was still crowded, so I was relieved that only a few people noticed the interruption and a lot of others remained dancing. Rich summoned one of the servers to bring me a glass of water, as he gently held my hand and brushed my hair out of my face. "Raquel, are you all right?" Rich asked nervously.

"Yes, Rich, thank you. I am sorry; I just got a little dizzy." Rich had no idea I was pregnant, and I certainly did not have any intention on telling him. "I think it was the champagne," I lied. "I really do not do too well with wine and champagne."

Rich looked at me enchantingly, still holding my hand. The server brought me a glass of water, and Siara was closely behind him.

"Raquel, what's wrong?" Siara asked concerned.

"Siara, I am fine, really I am. I think I am going to head home now, though," I replied.

"I can drive you home," Siara volunteered.

"No, no," Rich and I both said simultaneously.

"I will take her home," Rich offered.

Siara looked at me for approval.

"No, really, I am okay. Siara, I will call you later, okay?"

"Are you sure, Raquel?" Siara asked.

"Yes, and thanks so much, Siara."

"Okay," she replied hesitantly, and turned slowly to resume her interaction with the wedding guests.

All of the time Siara and I were engaged in conversation; Rich was lovingly stroking my hand. Rich seemed cool, but I was too emotionally involved with Clyde. I had no desire to explore anything with any other man.

"Rich, I am okay driving myself home."

"Raquel, why don't you just leave your car here and let me drive you home? I will check with Lance to make sure that it is ok for me to leave," Rich said.

"No, Rich, really; I will be fine. I do appreciate everything," hoping I had finally convinced him. I checked my watch, and it was approaching 5:30 PM My mind regressed back to Clyde.

"Ok, Raquel, if you insist. I will walk you to your car. I would appreciate if you gave me a call and let me know you are alright," Rich concluded. He reached in his pocket for his wallet, pulled out a card, and placed it in my hand. "Please call, Raquel," Rich pleaded.

"I will, Rich. Thanks again for a great time, and keeping me company," I said.

"The pleasure was all mine, Raquel." He then endeared me yet again with another kiss on my hand.

Damn! Clyde better watch out. This young guy has skills! I grabbed my purse, and Rich escorted me out of the church hall. As we made our way to my car, Rich kissed me on my cheek.

"I really like you, Raquel. Maybe we can have dinner before I return to D.C," Rich said.

I smiled at Rich, and got into my car as he secured my door.

"We'll see, Rich. I will give you a call. Please give Lance and Lacey my best regards."

"I will, Raquel." Rich paused for a few minutes as he gazed into my eyes. He then slowly turned around, and headed back to the reception. I watched Rich for a minute as my mind began to wonder. I then started my car, and finally headed home.

CHAPTER TWENTY EIGHT

During my ride home, all kinds of emotions raced through my head. Clyde dominated my myriad of thoughts. *What the hell was I going to do now?* I noticed the time on my clock radio, which illuminated 5:47 PM Clyde and Chloe were not going on a honeymoon, and Clyde insisted that he was coming to see me after his nuptials and reception were over. I don't know how he was going to pull that off on his wedding day, but he was sure he had everything under control. I really tried to dissuade him from coming, because I knew he and I would be too emotional, and we would probably end up in some massive argument. I certainly did not want that, but Clyde was adamant about coming over. No matter what happened, deep down inside, I really wanted to see his face tonight. I loved him, and nothing was going to ever change that.

Clyde is married now. Here I am again...alone, hurting, frustrated and rejected. Clyde claimed he loved me, but he did not love me enough **not** to marry Chloe. He had made all of these damn excuses about having to marry her. I'd hoped that he would not proceed with the wedding once I told him about the baby. Clyde claimed to have wanted this baby so desperately. I gave in to his pleas because I loved him so much. I did want to have his child, but I wanted us to be together.

I do not understand why I always fall in love with the wrong men. A lot of men hit on me, but I always seem to choose the wrong man. *What the hell was the matter with me?* Loud sirens and flashing lights distracted my thoughts. *Where are they going?* I wondered as a couple of police cars, and an ambulance flew past me at about 100 miles an hour. I was about ten minutes away from home, and could not wait to get home to soak in a warm bath and get myself together before Clyde got there. It would probably be a while before he got there, so at least I would be able to have my meditation time before he arrived.

As I approached a major intersection getting closer to my home, I could clearly see where the police cars and ambulance were heading. There was an accident, and it looked pretty bad. *Oh God, I hope no one got killed.* I prayed that no one I knew was involved. Thank God, I knew it was not my baby, Daniel Jr. because he was out of town with his godparents. And Lord, please don't let it be any of my family members. There were so many people out here that it looked like a parade! I could not even see the cars involved because of so many people. The police were directing traffic to a side street, in which I gladly obliged. I surely did not want to be caught up in that mess. I would wait and read about it in the paper or see it on the news. I just prayed for the people who were involved.

I finally made it home. As I proceeded to exit my car, I got another sharp pain in my stomach. *Oh Lord, what is going on?* I struggled to make it to my door and let myself in. As I headed to the living room sofa, I noticed my message light on my phone was beeping. I sat down on the sofa, which gave me a little relief from the pain in my stomach. *Lord, please don't let me lose this baby.* I needed to check my messages, because I knew Clyde was one of them. I sat still for a few minutes to allow the pain in my stomach to cease, and it does eventually. *Thank God!* I took my shoes off and headed upstairs to the bathroom to make sure that I was not spotting or anything because I didn't want to lose this baby.

I made it to the bathroom and checked myself. *Thank God, I was not spotting.* I prayed that my baby was okay, and myself, for that matter. The sharp pain seemed to dissipate. I still felt a bit strange, but at least I was no longer experiencing any excruciating pain in my stomach. I really could not explain the dim feeling that I felt, as if something was wrong.

As I made it to my bedroom to take off my clothes and prepare to take a warm bath; my clock radio on my nightstand startled me with a loud beep. It was six o'clock PM. I'd thought I had set my alarm for six o'clock AM; however, I'd set it to PM instead. I disabled the alarm on my clock, and retreated back into my bathroom to prepare for my bath.

I began to get undressed, and my slightly protruding stomach grabbed my attention. As I stared at my stomach in my bathroom mirror, I began to caress this new life I had growing inside of me.

"*I want you to know that mommy loves you, and I cannot wait to meet you,*" I confessed to my unborn child.

I turned on the bath water, and reached for my robe behind the bathroom door. I remembered that I had not checked my messages on my recorder, so I retreated back to my bedroom and sat down on my bed to listen to my messages. The message indicator reflected four messages.

"Hey, Momma. I'll be home tomorrow. I'm having a great time, and I am going to need twenty-five dollars for my football pictures tomorrow. I love you. Bye."

I was glad Daniel Jr. was having a good time. It was quiet with Daniel Jr. being gone the entire weekend, and I had missed him being home.

"Hey, girl, I am just calling to check on you. Call me when you get in," my sister, Rachel said.

"Hey, baby. How are both my babies?" Clyde said.

"Well baby, I am feeling real funny today. I don't know if I can go through with this. I can't keep my mind off of you, so I don't know how the hell I am going to do this. Raquel, I am sorry about taking you through this. Baby, I need you to know how very much I love you, and I cannot lose you. I won't lose you. You got that, Raquel? Okay, baby, I'll see you in a little while. I need to go handle this. I love you, Raquel, forever baby."

I had almost forgotten about the bath water running, and returned to the bathroom to turn off water.

Damn, Clyde! I am so sick of crying over him, over us. My eyes began to water, and I was unable to stop the tears. *What was he saying? I love his ass, and I hate that I do. Clyde sounded really confused and nervous.* It almost seemed like he was not ready to go through with his wedding. I hated to say it, but I'd hoped he did not go through with it. I did not want to hurt Chloe. She had done nothing to me, but Clyde and I belonged together! I'd just hoped that Chloe would understand that and deal with it.

There was one more message on my phone, and I attempted to gain my composure before proceeding to listen to it.

"Hey, Raquel, this is Linda." Linda was one of my girlfriends. "Girl, please call me as soon as you get in. Clyde was in a bad motorcycle accident on Forest Avenue. I'm sorry, girl. Call me."

Oh my God. Not Clyde. Oh God, please help me. Please let Clyde be okay. Please God, let him be all right.

I was shaking and crying uncontrollably. *This could not be happening.* I know this is God punishing me for seeing Clyde, and all of the other stupid things I've done in my life! *Lord, please forgive me; please forgive Clyde.*

I somehow managed to pick up the phone and call Linda back. No one answered. I wondered where she could be. I needed to get to Clyde. I needed to see him.

"*Help me, God!*" I pleaded. "*Please help me!*"

I scrambled around my room for something to put on, and slipped on a pair of jeans and a tank top. *This could not be happening. I can't lose Clyde!* I put on a pair of sandals, and almost fell running down the stairs while holding my stomach at the same time. *Where are my keys? I have got to calm down. Help me, Lord!* I located my keys on my dining room table where I had thrown them when I came in from the wedding.

I headed out of the door without even locking it behind me, and jumped in my car *and started driving. Where the hell was I going?*

Where the hell was Linda? Oh my God, I know it was not that accident I saw coming home from the wedding. Oh God, no! I was still shaking uncontrollably. *Clyde could not die.* Surely, I would die. *What about our baby?*

I finally made it to the intersection of 18th and Wilder. *This is the accident scene I saw coming home from Lance and Lacy's wedding! Forest Avenue was the next street over!* There were people everywhere. I had never seen so many people in my life. Police were everywhere. I saw people moaning and crying. Every one looked sad.

The police were directing traffic to a side street, in which I nervously obliged. I managed to find an obscure parking place, and put my car in park, turned off the engine, and jumped out. There were people staring at me, shaking their heads. *Why were they looking at me?. And why were they shaking their heads?*

I spotted Linda. *Why in the hell was she crying?* Linda noticed me and ran towards me, along with a few of her acquaintances, whom were staring at me pitifully.

"Raquel!" Linda screamed.

"Linda, is it Clyde?" I wanted to know.

"Yes, Raquel, it's Clyde. They said he is not going to make it. I am so sorry, Raquel," Linda struggled to get out, while sobbing.

"Where is he, Linda?" I asked hysterically.

"Raquel, please don't go over there," Linda pleaded.

Linda and her entourage were trying desperately to discourage me from going to Clyde, and Linda attempted to restrain me as well.

"Linda, let me go!" I screamed. "Please, Linda, let go of me!" I repeated adamantly. "I have to see him!" I continued to yell while sobbing inconsolably.

"Okay, Raquel. I'll take you over there, but they have probably already put him in the ambulance," Linda said, trying to offer me some sort of comfort. "Raquel, Chloe is over there, too," Linda informed me. I didn't want to cause any disturbance, or have any encounter with Chloe, but I had to see Clyde.

"What about their wedding?" I asked Linda.

"Raquel, people are saying that Clyde did not show up for the wedding, and he was on his way to see you," Linda explained.

"What?" I said, trying to gasp for air. *Clyde did not get married!*

"He was coming to see you."

"Linda, are you sure the wedding did not take place?" I asked.

"Yes, I am sure. That's what everyone out here is talking about."

Without warning, I broke away from Linda and took off running towards the scene of the accident.

"Raquel, wait, please wait!" Linda was close behind me yelling at the top of her lungs.

It seemed like I was running in slow motion. All eyes were on me. I could hear some of the crowd whispering as I ran past them.

"There *she* goes."

"That's Raquel."

"That's the chick Clyde was seeing."

Right now I did not give a damn about the whisperings. They could talk all they wanted as far as I was concerned. The only thing I was worried about was Clyde and getting to him. Somehow I made my way through the crowd of people, police, and paramedics. Then I saw him, and I was frozen. *"Oh God, Clyde!" I* screamed.

Clyde's body lay there in the middle of the street lifeless. I could not believe what I was seeing. I had to have been having a nightmare. I heard more screaming and sobbing, and saw it was Chloe crying in an older man's arm. She was screaming, "Why couldn't it have been her?"

Incidentally, my heart ached for her pain as well. I made my way just a little closer to Clyde, trying to prevent any further disturbances. *Where was his arm?* One of his arms was severed completely off. His face was in tact, but his body was all twisted. I was frozen again and could not move nor speak. My body began to shake. Just as I was about to pass out, someone caught me before I hit the pavement. That was all I remembered, until waking up the next day in the hospital.

CHAPTER TWENTY NINE

I woke up in the hospital the next day surrounded by people. My sisters, Sashe and Selena were there. Daniel Jr. was also here, and my girlfriend Linda.

"Raquel, how are you feeling?" Sashe asked pitifully.

"Rachel and Mark are on their way here from Daytona," she added.

"I'm okay, sis," I managed to respond.

I did not need to ask about Clyde. I could tell by the looks on my two sisters' faces, and Daniel Jr. that Clyde did not survive the accident. But I was praying for a miracle, even though Clyde looked so badly when I saw him at the accident scene. His arm was severed, and he was unconscious. There was no sign of life. I could not resist the urge.

"Sashe, is Clyde dead?" I asked without warning.

"Yes, Raquel, he did not make it."

"Oh my God! No, no, no! Oh Lord, please help me," I cried.

"Raquel, you have got to calm down," Selena told me firmly.

Daniel Jr. just sat there stoically. He was really fond of Clyde.

"Yes Raquel, please calm down," Linda pleaded with tears in her eyes.

I tried my best to calm down, with little success.

"Raquel, the doctor will have to medicate you again, so please try to calm down," Sashe pleaded, almost sobbing.

Sashe and Selena knew Clyde and about our relationship, but did not approve of it. I knew that, but I loved Clyde. They knew that too, so they did not pressure me about it. I loved them for that. Rachel was adamantly against the relationship. She did not want me to get hurt, and I know Sashe and Selena felt the same as well, but Rachel was always scolding me about Clyde.

When I told Rachel that I was pregnant with Clyde's baby, she had a fit.

"Raquel, I cannot believe you want to have a baby with his ass. You are struggling taking care of Daniel with no daddy."

"Rachel, please, Clyde will be there for this baby," I would plead with her.

"Yeah right," Rachel would say. Neither Sashe, nor Selena knew about my pregnancy, until now.

The thought of the baby jolted me back into reality. "Is my baby okay?" I asked.

Sashe looked really upset and nervous. She turned to Selena seemingly waiting for her to respond. Before, Selena could respond, a man who appeared to be a doctor walked in.

"Hi, Ms. West, I am Dr. Tyler," he introduced himself.

Yes, doctor, how's my baby?" I asked without warning.

"Dr. Tyler glanced over to Sashe and Selena with a perplexed expression.

"Ms. West, you need to get some rest. You have been through a traumatic experience."

"Please, just tell me doctor, that my baby is okay," I pleaded.

Daniel, Jr. exited the room. *Oh my God! I lost the baby?* I could sense Daniel Jr.'s sadness, and he could not stand to see me emotional or crying.

"Ms. West, I am sorry, but you were in your first trimester, which is the most delicate time for a pregnancy. The baby did not survive," Dr. Tyler confirmed.

"Your fall caused severe trauma to the womb, and the baby had no chance of survival. We had no choice but to terminate the gestation," Dr. Tyler concluded.

"What?" I screamed. Sashe and Selena came over in an attempt to comfort me.

"I lost the baby, too?" I began to sob uncontrollably.

Linda exited the room to comfort Daniel Jr. I cried like a baby both into Sashe and Selena's arms. *"What am I going to do? I've lost Clyde and our baby. Oh God, please help me,"* I pleaded with God.

"Ms. West, I am terribly sorry for your loss," Dr. Tyler said. "There was nothing else we could do," he explained.

I continued to cry hysterically. Sashe and Selena tried to calm me down to no avail. Dr. Tyler summoned his nurse to give me a sedative to help calm me down.

"Ms. West, I know this is very difficult for you, but you have to focus on yourself now and your health, please. Your blood pressure had elevated to a dangerous level, and we did manage to get it under control; however, we have to keep it that way, okay," Dr. Tyler tried to reason with me. I am going to have the nurse give you a sedative to calm you and help you sleep tonight, because I don't feel like you are ready to go home just yet. You are going to get through this."

"Whatever we can do to assist you, please don't hesitate to contact me."

My hysterical cries had repelled to whimpering while still attempting to be comforted by my sisters. Dr. Tyler requested to see Selena outside as he exited my room. The nurse approached me to give me the sedative.

"Raquel, the nurse needs you to cooperate as she gives you the sedative," Sashe said while holding my head into her arms.

"Okay," was all I could get out in response to Sashe's empathetic plea.

The nurse made her way to the right side of my bed to administer the shot. Without warning, and surely no time for me to resist, she poked my arm, and it was all over.

"Ms. West, you need to rest. Call me if you need anything. My name is Shannon," the nurse said. She then stroked my face gently and told me everything was going to be all right, and exited my room.

CHAPTER THIRTY

It had been seven days since Clyde was killed in the motorcycle accident. His funeral was today. I had come home from the hospital five days ago. I was so heartbroken for losing Clyde, and our baby; I blamed myself. I'd learned that Clyde did not show up for his wedding, and in fact, he was en route to see me when he had the accident.

His best friend, Tim, whom was his partner at the barbershop, had come to see me a couple of days ago. He confirmed for me that Clyde was en route to my home. Tim was a cool guy. He and Clyde were like brothers. They both had migrated to the Tampa Bay Area from Ft. Lauderdale, Florida about ten years ago and opened up *Clyde's Barbershop.*

"Raquel, I want you to know that Clyde loved you very much," Tim assured me. Yes, he loved Chloe, too, but he definitely had a different love for you," he explained. "He just did not know how to break it off with Chloe. He felt obligated to her. He told me that he was not letting you go for anything, and he was very excited about the baby, too. He wanted you to have his first son," he told me." Tim tried to smile through a faint tear that made its way down his cheek.

I finally came back to life after listening to Tim attempt to console me about Clyde. I gave Tim a heartfelt hug and told him to be strong, and let him know how much I appreciated him coming to see me on Clyde's behalf.

"I almost forgot Raquel, this is for you," Tim said and handed me an envelope. "Clyde took out an insurance policy when he found out you were pregnant. He wanted to make sure he had some type of security in place for you and the baby if anything was to happen to him," Tim said.

"What is it Tim?" I asked.

"Just open it when I leave Raquel. Clyde wanted you to have it," Tim concluded.

"I am going to miss my man, Raquel," Tim said amidst masculine sobs.

"I know, Tim. I miss him terribly, but we have got to be strong for Clyde," I said, trying to encourage myself as well.

"Yeah, you're right, Raquel."

"Take care of yourself Raquel," Tim says and exits the door.

God was punishing me for my sins. I should have broken it off with Clyde a long time ago, and maybe he would still be alive. I knew he had a woman! They were going to be married! But, I was totally swept off my feet by Clyde and eventually fell deeply in love with him. He was everything I had wanted in man, and he made me feel so special, even though he was with someone else.

How could I be so foolish and allow myself to become involved with him? I knew better, but I was so vulnerable and broken inside from the pain Daniel Jr.'s father had inflicted on me. Clyde eliminated all of my pain, and I felt like I was re-incarnated when I met him. I never thought I could fall in love with another man, but I did fall in love with Clyde. I'd loved Daniel Sr., but he never reciprocated it genuinely to me. Clyde loved me. I felt his love. I felt his love when he talked to me; when he would do special things for me, surprise me with gifts, take me out, and especially when we made love. Clyde and I had something special, and I would never forget him.

I had almost forgotten about the envelope Tim left me from Clyde. As I begin to open up the envelope, I immediately realized it was a check. *Laser Life Insurance, Paid to the order of Raquel West, the sum of $25,000.00. Oh my God!* Clyde had left me $25,000.00! I just began to cry.

CHAPTER THIRTY ONE

I had decided not to attend Clyde's funeral out of respect for Chloe. I knew I would lose it. I had to keep myself together and get stronger in order to survive this myself. I did make myself go to the funeral home today to see Clyde and tell him goodbye. I was going to go early, with hopes to avoid the family. I also wanted to spend some time with him alone. I did not know how I would act seeing Clyde lying in that casket, but I had to go tell him goodbye, and that I loved him, and how sorry I was.

So many things were going through my cluttered mind, but Clyde was the one thing that was constant. I felt so guilty that Clyde was no longer here. I was on my knees praying every day for the past week, pleading with God for forgiveness and strength. I just could not believe that I would never see or feel Clyde again. I thought about his accident.

I had so many questions. Was he in pain when he was killed? Did he suffer? Did he feel anything? Was it an instant death on impact? How long did he live after the accident? If he did survive at all after he was hit, did he think of me; did he call my name?

I thought about since he did not wed Chloe, and was on his way to see me, would we have finally been together as we should have been. Would Clyde and I have married and raised our baby together? Was he coming to tell me that he could not live without me, and our baby?

I could not believe that Clyde did not go through with the wedding. The last time I had been with him, he gave me no indication that he was not going to show up for his wedding. However, he was really quiet that evening. I suspected Clyde was thinking about many things, and I allowed him time for his thoughts.

My telephone rang constantly all morning, as I prepared to go view Clyde's body.

"Hi, Raquel," my other half was on the other end of the phone.

"Hi, Rachel," I replied, trying to keep calm and appear strong. I did not want Rachel to worry so much about me.

"I am just calling to check on you. Are you going to the funeral?"

"No, I am not going, but I am going to view his body."

"Is Sashe or Selena going to go with you?"

"No, I'd rather go alone. I'll be okay, Rachel."

"I don't think you should go by yourself, Raquel."

"Rachel, I need this time alone with Clyde. I am not going to stay long. I promise you; I will be fine."

"You sure? What about you friend Linda? Why don't you have her take you?"

"Rachel, I don't want anyone to take me; I want to go by myself," I replied insistently.

"Okay, Raquel. Please call me when you get home."

"I will. Thanks."

We ended the call. Well, that's one down and two more to go.

My sisters and I were very close, so I did expect to hear from Sashe and Selena as well. I did appreciate their concern and loved them for it, but I really needed to get through this alone, without any inter-rogation and pressure from anyone.

As I prepared to shower and get dressed, the phone rang again. I wanted to ignore it but when I checked the caller ID, I could see it was Janine, Daniel, Jr.'s godmother.

Daniel Jr. was over there for the weekend, so it was probably him calling to check on me.

"Ma," a husky male voice said on the other end of the phone.

"Yes, how are you, Daniel?" I replied.

"Fine. How are *you* doing?" Daniel Jr. asked as if he were the par-ent.

"I am okay, Daniel. When are you coming home?" I inquired, try-ing to change the subject.

"I'll be home tomorrow, Ma."

"Are you going to Clyde's funeral today?" Daniel, Jr. asked hesi-tantly.

"No, but I am trying to get ready now to go view his body. Did you want to go, Daniel?" I asked.

Daniel, Jr. had been quite fond of Clyde, and I knew his heart was hurting over Clyde's death, although he would never let me know.

"Wade and I already went to see him today."

What? I could not believe that Daniel Jr. took it upon himself to go to the funeral home to see Clyde. I knew Daniel Jr. liked Clyde, but I was really shocked that he thought enough of Clyde to go view his body.

Daniel Jr. had never liked any other man I dated after his dad and I broke up. But he did like Clyde. That was even more apparent now.

"So you went to see Clyde, Daniel?"

"Yeah, Momma," he replied, trying to sound nonchalant, but I could detect sadness in his voice.

I felt like crying again, but I recited the name of *Jesus* repeatedly in my heart for strength.

"How does he look?" I asked hesitantly.

"He looked like he was sleeping, Ma," he replied, somewhat irritable. I could tell he did not want me to continue with my interrogation, so I let him be.

"You know, Daniel, Clyde was really fond of you. I appreciate you going and paying your respects to him."

"I know, Ma." We both remain silent on the phone for about ten seconds.

"Okay, Ma, I gotta' go. I will be home tomorrow," he assured me.

"Be careful and stay out of trouble. I love you, Daniel."

"Love you, too," he replied and hangs up.

As I stand there numb for a few minutes, I glanced around the room and noticed the time on my clock radio was 11:27 AM. Clyde's viewing was at one o'clock, and his – home-going service was scheduled for three o'clock.

I proceeded to my bathroom to shower and get ready to go to the funeral home. I turned on the water in the shower and stooped down near the tub to run my fingers through the water checking for a suitable temperature. When the water temperature reached a tolerable temperature for me, I slowly removed my robe and stepped in the shower. The water felt soothing on my body.

As the water trickled down my back, I began to think about all of the tears I had cried for so long. So much pain… when was it going to end? Well, it was not happening today. Before I knew it, tears became immersed in the water, as they flowed all over my body. The flow of them seemed even more than the water coming from the shower. I slid down in the tub in a fetal position and allowed the "cleansing" to take its course.

CHAPTER THIRTY TWO

I must have sat weeping in the tub for at least thirty minutes. Eventually, I somehow solicited God for some inner strength to get up and caress my body with my bath cloth and some soap. By the time I managed to get out of the shower to get dressed, it was 12:15 PM I had to hurry, because I wanted to make it there before other family and friends came. I was not going to attend the service, so something simple would suffice.

I pondered through my closet a few minutes trying to conjure up something to put on. I pulled out a pair of jeans. Clyde loved me in these jeans. I hurriedly slipped on the jeans, and looked for a nice blouse to accent my jeans. I pulled out a freshly dry cleaned, sleek, melon colored blouse to wear. That would work. I detached the dry cleaning ticket in the collar of the blouse and slipped it on. All looked well, except for accessories. I reached for my gold Donna Karen belt, while also slipping my feet into some comfortable, casual mules. I went to my jewelry box to find a necklace to complement my attire. I pulled out a 1/2-carat diamond necklace that Clyde had bought me last year for Christmas. I placed the necklace around my neck and secured the clasp. I checked my appearance in the mirror while affixing my belt through the hoops in my jeans. Everything was fitting perfectly. Thank goodness!

I had micro braids in my hair for the first time ever, and I was really pleased with them. The young lady that did them did a great job, and they made me look at least five years younger. They were very convenient; however, I was dreading having to take them out. I had only had them a couple of weeks, so they were still pretty fresh.

I sprayed a little oil sheen on my braids to give them some shine, and I massaged my scalp with some conditioning cream. I did not wear a lot of makeup, so eyeliner and lipstick would complete me. Normally I would only wear a little concealer, if I were going out; however, my face looked drained from crying so much, so I opted to wear it. When I finished, I really did not look bad at all. Clyde would have liked it, and that's all that mattered to me.

I glanced over to my alarm clock on my dresser, and it was 12:27 PM, so I grabbed my purse, keys, and some tissue out of the bathroom, and ran down the stairs. Out the door, I went and jumped into my new red Dodge Mustang. It was my first brand new car ever. Clyde had given me the down payment to purchase it.

My heart and mind were both racing. I really had to calm myself down. I was hoping Chloe would not be there yet. I did not want to intrude and cause any problems for Chloe or anyone else for that matter.

I had seen Chloe different places from time to time, but I never had any intention on confronting her about Clyde. That was not my place, and I just did not believe in that.

What Clyde and I had was between he and I, and he would be the one I confronted about anything. Chloe had done nothing to me, and as long as she stayed in her place, she would not have any problems with me.

I don't know if she knew about me or not before Clyde was killed, but I was sure she knew or had heard about me by now.

There was one incident where I was invited to a party at a club, and Chloe was there, too, with some of her friends. Every now and then I would catch her staring me down. I figured that maybe she knew or had found out about me, but she never confronted me, so we both continued to party without incident. I had asked Clyde if she knew about he and I, and he told me she had no idea.

I wondered about that. How could a woman not know her man was cheating on her or feeling another woman? Clyde and I spent a lot of time together. Not as much as I would have liked, but it was enough time that if I was Chloe, I would've certainly questioned my man's whereabouts. Then again, Clyde's ass was good. He always used to tell me that he handled his business. In that, he was referring to keeping Chloe in check and both of us happy.

I finally made it to the funeral home. There were a few cars in the parking lot. I glanced at my clock in my dashboard and it read 1:17 PM. Well, the viewing had just started, so hopefully there were not a lot of people in there.

I parked my car and took a deep breath. *Lord, I sure hope Chloe is not here yet. Raquel, you have got to keep it together!* I walked to the entrance of the funeral home, and two distinguished men with black suits greeted me at the entrance.

"How are you doing, ma'am?" They both said simultaneously and opened the door for me.

"Fine, thank you," I replied nervously.

I walked in trembling, and the first thing I noticed was a beautiful pearl white casket trimmed in gold in a room down the hall. Flowers surrounded the casket; I could see them even from a distance. *That must be Clyde.* I then spotted the devotion book for guests to sign, and a sign that read *Mr. Clyde Brown.* An arrow pointed in the direction of the casket I noticed upon my entrance.

I walked up to the guest book and paused for a moment pondering whether or not I should sign the book. I decided to just sign my name. A tear appeared out of nowhere, so I pulled a tissue out of my purse to dab my eyes. I was determined to be strong for Clyde.

As I began to walk down the hall towards Clyde's casket, about half the way there, I heard what appeared to be a woman weeping. It sounded like a puppy whimpering.

I really did not want to cause Chloe any more heartache than what she was already going through. I had to say goodbye to Clyde, no matter what. I made it to the entrance of the door where Clyde was, and I saw a woman seated in a chair pulled right next to Clyde's casket. She was at the head of the casket with her head in her lap, weeping. Sure enough, it was Chloe. It seemed as if my heart stopped for a minute. I had to figure out what to do. My heart went out to Chloe. I could feel her pain and agony. She must have really loved Clyde, but so did I. I pondered the thought of not even going up to the casket, so that I would not disturb Chloe, but quickly dismissed that thought.

I slowly walked up to the casket. It did not even appear as if Chloe knew I was there, or anyone else for that matter. Her head remained in her lap. I really felt sorry for her, and knew I had to keep it together. I just stared at Clyde. He looked good, just like he was sleeping, as Daniel Jr. had said. He was dressed in a nice blue suit, silk shirt and tie.

I glanced over at Chloe, and she still held her head down. I really wanted to kiss Clyde goodbye, but I refrained from doing that out of respect for Chloe. Silently, in my heart, I told Clyde how much I loved him, and I was going to miss him and how sorry I was. I thanked him for loving me. I also told him I would never, ever forget him. I kept my composure, and I slowly turned to exit.

I don't know what made me say it, but before I proceeded to leave, I turned to Chloe, who still had her head hung low, and said, "I am sorry, Chloe."

She brought her head up and looked me in my face, while still weeping and trembling; she mustered out the words, "Thanks for coming."

I stood there stoical for about ten seconds. Chloe really did not have any idea who I was. Or could it be because of her grieving over Clyde, she could not see anyone right now? In any event, I was relieved, because I sure did not want any type of confrontation with her. For some strange reason, my heart really went out to her. I finally turned around, made my exit out of the room, praying that I would not lose it, and make it home safely.

CHAPTER THIRTY THREE

I don't know how I did it, but I did. I arrived home in one piece after leaving the funeral home from bidding my Clyde farewell. Amazingly, I was pretty calm, or at least calmer than I had been the past week. I had cried a river since learning of Clyde's death, and I had lost Clyde and I baby

I was so tired of crying and hurting. I did not know how I was going to continue on, but I did know I had to continue. After seeing Clyde in that casket, the reality of him being gone, and me never seeing him, talking to him, touching him, or him touching me ever again made me numb.

I realized that I had to make some changes in my life. I wanted to leave this damn city for one thing. It was too painful for me to stay there. I needed a fresh start, and I wanted that. I just did not know where to start. Also, I knew Daniel Jr. would not like the idea of moving to another city or state. But he would have to deal with it, because there was no way I could remain here. Besides, I needed to get Daniel Jr. away from here, too.

He had continued giving me a lot of problems and getting into trouble. I was not going to lose my son to the system!

I started planning for my transition, a new start, and a new life. I had been talking with Rachel and Mark quite often about me moving to Daytona where they lived.

The plan was for me to move in with them for a while, until I found a job, and then move into my own place. I talked to my mother about my decision to move to Daytona with Rachel and Mark. She was not too happy about it, but she understood and accepted my decision. I had also talked to Sashe and Selena about me moving, and they were receptive and hesitant at the same time. They understood why I wanted to make the transition and get a new start in life. After all that I had been through, they were not happy about another one of their sisters moving away.

I remember when Rachel and Mark had made the decision to leave Tampa. Sashe and Selena were not happy about Rachel leaving at all. I was heartbroken. Rachel was my other half. How in the hell was I going to make it without her? Even though Rachel and I argued and had our differences, we were extremely close. Our arguing was always her telling me about my life, or vice versa, but that never came between the bond that we definitely shared.

Rachel was always worried about me because I was the single

sister. Rachel and Selena were both married, and Sashe was in a common law marriage.

"Raquel, you and Daniel Jr. need to just come on and move here to Daytona," Rachel had told me. "I know you are still hurting about Clyde, but you have got to go on, Raquel."

"I know, girl I am so sick of this place. Daniel Jr. is driving me crazy," I replied. "I had already been thinking about leaving here anyway."

"You can stay with Mark and I, until you find a job, and get your own place. Clyde left you more than enough to start over somewhere else," Rachel said.

I really missed Rachel, and she was right. I needed a change. Losing Clyde was the final straw for me. I was devastated and was so guilt ridden over his death. I was not getting any younger. I wanted to settle down someday, and have a happy, peaceful life. I had faith that would happen, eventually. I was so sick of these sorry ass men, and this sorry ass city!

"It's really nice here, Raquel. I am so glad Mark and I decided to leave Tampa."

Rachel and her husband Mark had relocated to Daytona, Florida about six months ago.

"Yeah, I know what you mean, sis. I really miss you a lot. I am coming, but I have to get everything in order here."

"What is it that you have to do Raquel?" Rachel asked.

"Well, I need to finish this session in school and talk to Daniel Jr. You know he is going to be tripping, but I need to get him out of here anyway."

"Yeah, you do, with all of the trouble he keeps getting into," Rachel said.

"I know, and he is stressing me out," I replied.

"Have you heard from his drop-shot ass daddy?" Rachel asked.

"Yes, he calls occasionally."

"How much time does he have left?" Rachel asks.

"I am not really sure. He will never tell me, you know that," I reply.

"Girl, do not even waste your time talking to that drop-shot."

"Does he talk to Daniel Jr.?"

"Sometimes, but Daniel Jr. never wants to get on the phone and talk to him when he calls. I have to make him talk to him and let him know that no matter what, unfortunately, he is still his dad. Daniel Jr. also knows that his dad will get on him about the trouble he has been getting into."

"Well, that's what the Daniel Sr. gets! He is so damn busy trying to play daddy everywhere else, now Daniel Jr. doesn't want to be bothered with his trifling ass. Daniel Jr. is almost 16 years old now!"

"It's too late for Daniel Sr. to play daddy with him now!" Rachel said.

"I know, girl." Daniel Jr. has a lot of hurt inside of him for everything he witnessed between his dad and I. Our constant fighting and cursing each other out around him. I blame myself for that, too."

"Yeah, but it was Daniel Sr's. damn fault!" Rachel concludes.

"Let me do some planning, sis, and I'll get back with you. I am definitely coming though."

"Okay, call me back. Mark will come and move you."

"I know, and I appreciate that so much." "Love ya," I conclude.

"Love you, too," Rachel finally hangs up.

Damn, I am getting my ass out of here! Rachel was so right; it's time for me to go. No more procrastinating. I know Daniel Jr. is going to give me a hard time, but that is too bad! He'll just have to deal with it. I am so sick of him getting in and out of trouble, staying out all night, and having me worried sick about him. It was amazing he was still attending school! I love him to death! God knows I would not be able to deal with anything happening to him. And me, I definitely need a new start.

I cannot stay here and mourn Clyde's death the rest of my life. I have to get on with my life.

CHAPTER THIRTY-FOUR

It took me a year to complete my transitional plans to Daytona Beach, Florida. During that time, I did everything I could to convince Daniel Jr. that the move would be great for us. A chance for us to get a new lease on life and meet new people, but Daniel Jr. fought me to the end about the move. He adamantly did not want to leave Tampa.

"All of my friends are here," he had explained.

"You will meet new friends and your friends here can come and visit, but we are leaving tomorrow Daniel!" I had told him.

Daniel Jr. and I things were all packed for our move to Daytona, Florida. I was so excited and happy to be leaving what I considered a hellhole. I had so many bitter memories, and I was ready to leave them all behind and embark on a new life. It was Friday morning, and Mark would be here early tomorrow morning to move Daniel Jr. and me to Daytona. I had said all of my goodbyes to friends, family, and co-workers.

Daniel Jr. was still very angry about moving. He had been getting in a lot of trouble in school, and recently had been suspended for smoking marijuana. I had hoped that he did not "pull any stunts" as I was trying to get us the hell out of here! Of course he did, and I surely thought I would lose my mind!

Daniel Jr. did not come home Friday night. I had called everywhere and went riding around the town looking for him. I had even called the jail and juvenile center looking for him. I was a basket case. He knew we were all packed to leave in the morning. I couldn't believe he was doing this crap to me!

I called Rachel to tell her about Daniel Jr. missing, and she told me not to panic.

"He'll be home in the morning. Where else does he have to go?" Rachel said.

"I don't know, Rachel. He was so adamant about not moving to Daytona, and I am so worried about him. I *have* to leave tomorrow. Everything is all planned."

"Raquel, calm down. Mark will be there in the morning as scheduled, and Daniel Jr. will be home, okay?" Rachel said, attempting to relieve me.

"Okay, Rachel. Thanks. I'll see you tomorrow evening," I replied tiredly.

It was 10:35 PM, and Daniel Jr.'s ass did not even have the decency to call me and let me know that he was all right. I was going to tear his ass up when he got home!

I was so furious with Daniel Jr! I lit a cigarette, not knowing where to turn now. I wandered around my home checking to make sure I had everything packed and was clean. The place was immaculate; I had done a good job. I made it to my bedroom and lied across my bed, the only thing still in tact, and I began to pray.

Lord, please let Daniel Jr. be okay, and please send him home right now.

I was so exhausted from packing and worrying about Daniel Jr. and did not realize I had dozed off until the phone rang.

"Ma, I am all right," Daniel Jr. said on the other end of the phone.

"Daniel, where the hell are you?"

"I am staying with some friends," Daniel Jr. replied.

"Daniel!" I screamed into the phone. "Get your ass home, now!"

"Ma, stop yelling. I am not coming home. I am not moving to Daytona," he said defiantly. I thought I was going to faint.

"Daniel," I pleaded. "Please don't do this; you know we have to leave! Everything is all packed and set to go!" "Mark will be here early in the morning. If you do not bring your ass home now, I am going to call the police to find you, and I mean that!" I screamed.

"Ma, Uncle Carlos said I can stay here with him, and that I do not have to move to Daytona with you."

Carlos was my younger brother. Why would he tell Daniel, Jr. this? He knew I could not, and would not leave Daniel Jr. My child was going with me, even if I have to tie his ass up in the back of the U-Haul!

"Daniel, I don't care what Carlos says; you are **not** staying here. I am your mother, and you are coming with me!"

"Ma, please. I love you, but I am not coming home. Please don't worry about me. I am going to stay with Uncle Carlos. He is going to call you in the morning."

"Daniel, Daniel!" I screamed into the phone, but he had already hung up!

My God; what am I going to do? I could not just leave Daniel Jr. here and move to another city! I could not believe Daniel Jr. was doing this to me! I had to leave in the morning. I had no means of staying beyond tomorrow. Everything was planned and packed, and I had to be out of here tomorrow.

CHAPTER THIRTY FIVE

I decided to call my brother Carlos.

"Hello," Carlos answered lethargically.

"Carlos, this is Raquel."

"Raquel, what is the matter?"

"Carlos, you know that I am leaving tomorrow morning for Daytona, and Daniel Jr. refuses to come home. You know he's been fighting me on this move, and now he is telling me that you said he could stay here in Tampa with you!"

"Raquel, calm down. I did tell him that," Carlos said defensively.

"Carlos, you know he cannot stay here with you. I am his mother; he needs to be with me." I began to cry. "Why would you even tell him he could stay with you? You're just encouraging him to fight me even more on this."

"Raquel, you know that's not what I was trying to do. The boy has been driving you crazy. Why don't you just go ahead to Daytona and settle down. Get your life together and let Daniel Jr. stay with me. He will be all right."

"Carlos, you know I can't do that. I would be worried sick about him."

"Well, what are you going to do, Raquel? You know how he is; he's not coming home. He told me that. He can stay with me. You know it's just me in this three bedroom house," Carlos explained.

"He knows I don't play with his ass and that will give you some time to go and get yourself situated without worrying about him."

I listened to Carlos with reservations; yet facing the reality that Daniel Jr. was not coming home. "Carlos, what about school?"

"Raquel, I will make sure he goes to school."

"What about him getting sick and eating properly? You would have to make sure he eats properly and healthy," I continued.

"Raquel, he will be fine," Carlos said. "If he gets sick or anything, I will contact you." Carlos said convincingly. "Get some rest, Raquel. I'll call you in the morning before you leave," Carlos concluded.

"Thanks, Carlos. Please take care of my baby," I reply.

"Good night, Raquel."

"Good night, Carlos." We both hang up.

It hurt me so bad to have to leave my baby, but I comforted myself with concluding that Carlos was right. I really needed to go and get my life and my mind together. I knew that Carlos would take care of Daniel Jr. Quite frankly, as much as it killed me to leave my baby, I thought that perhaps he would be better off there with Carlos... at least until I had got myself together. I needed some sanctity, and I was not going to get it here!

There were too many memories that I wanted to forget. I felt like I deserved better, and I knew I could certainly do better. I was fearful, but my faith was in God. I really had no plan of action, no job, nothing planned, but I knew somehow, someway things would work out for me.

CHAPTER THIRTY SIX

Mark arrived to pick me up about 9:30 in the morning with the U-Haul truck. I was all packed and ready to get the hell out of here to begin a new life. On the other hand, I was sad about Daniel Jr. not coming with me. I was so drained with everything! I simply had no energy, or strength to fight with him anymore about coming with me. I had been fighting with him about this transition since I told him a year ago, and he had simply worn me out. It was a difficult decision for me to make to leave the only home I'd ever known. My only consolation was that there had to be a better life!

"Raquel, you ready to go?" Mark asked. "Yes, I am Mark," I replied.

Mark was really a good guy. He was a big guy in stature, and his heart was just as big. Mark was one of the most genuine, compassionate, and caring men I'd ever known. I know this is why Rachel fell in love with him, and she really needed a man like Mark.

Mark took care of Rachel, and he loved my sister. I was so glad he was with Rachel. He and I were very close. Since he had been married to Rachel, which was about six years now, it was like I was married to him too, because he was the only man I could count on to help me with anything.

Mark was always encouraging me and telling me how beautiful and intelligent his wife (Rachel) and I were, and that we deserved the best, and did not, nor should not ever tolerate any shit from a man!

Of course, he was always concerned about me, because he knew how close Rachel and I were. Mark was always scolding me about my love life, and the relationships I had succumbed to. He was really disappointed, particularly about my relationship with Clyde.

"Raquel, don't you think you deserve better than this?" he would scold me. You do not have to share another man! If he cannot commit to you and you only, drop his ass!" Mark would tell me.

"Where is Daniel, Jr.?" Mark asked puzzled when he noticed he was nowhere in sight.

"He ran away and refused to come home. Thank God he is with Carlos. I talked with Carlos last night, and he told me that Daniel Jr. was all right, and was staying with him. So, Daniel Jr won't be going," I concluded feeling defeated and softly started to cry just thinking of him not going with me.

"Raquel, don't worry about Daniel Jr. He'll be all right. Carlos will keep him in line. You just need to come on and get on with your life. Daniel Jr. is at that rebellious stage, but he is going to be okay," Mark replied.

"Thanks, Mark, for coming to get me."

I was trying to move on and not think about Daniel Jr. not coming with me. I just needed to get the hell out of here, and that was exactly what I was going to do. My only consolation about my son was that he would eventually join me in Daytona. I was going to get a job, a nice place to stay, and come back and get my child.

"You know Rachel is excited about you coming," Mark said, trying to cheer me up.

"I know, and I am so glad to be getting the hell out of here."

"So everything is packed and ready to go, right, Raquel?"

"Yes, we can start loading up."

"Let's do this." Mark smiled.

CHAPTER THIRTY SEVEN

Mark and I had packed the U-Haul truck in three hours. I had given all of my furniture and appliances away. The only big thing I kept was my bedroom set, because I needed something to sleep on. Mark and Rachel had a spare room, which they graciously allowed me to stay in. The only thing Mark and I had to pack was my bedroom set, which consisted of a queen size bed, a dresser with mirror, and two night stands. I still had my clothes, various personal and sentimental small items that I had kept and were taking with me. I had given Daniel Jr.'s entire bedroom set away, because there was nowhere to put it in Mark and Rachel's home. I was going to get him a new set eventually. Daniel Jr. would have slept on an air mattress in Mark and Rachel's den, which was what Daniel Jr. had suggested anyway. Mark and Rachel had agreed to that. All of Daniel Jr.'s personal items would go in my room.

I had not planned on staying with Mark and Rachel too long anyway. My plan was to get myself to Daytona and start looking for a job right away. As soon as I landed a job, I would find an apartment. Since Daniel Jr. was not joining me immediately, it would give me more time to concentrate on my job search, and find a place to stay. I would not have to worry about finding him a school and enrolling him right away. Rachel had checked several high schools out for Daniel Jr. to attend. So, I had to decide on which one before Daniel Jr. got here.

My mindset was firm, that no matter what, I would be returning to Tampa to get my son in three months! I was sick about leaving him behind, but Carlos and Mark were right. I had planned everything for a year, and my time was up with all the preparations I had made. I could not delay my transition any longer. Most importantly, I was ready.

Mark was finishing up ensuring that everything was securely packed in the truck. I had finished cleaning up and making sure that I had got everything. I glanced around the empty townhouse once more. I had already had my time of reminiscing, and it was simply time for me to leave.

I gropingly made my way to the front door, exited the townhouse, and locked the door with my key.

Mark had already started the truck.

"It was a done deal," as Mark would say. I was out of here. I made my way to the passenger side of the truck and got in.

"You ready?" Mark said reassuringly.

"Ready," I affirmed.

CHAPTER THIRTY EIGHT

Mark and I finally had left Tampa about two o'clock in the afternoon. Carlos had called before we left, and suggested I come by to see Daniel Jr. before I left. He promised he would make sure he was there! I was happy about that, and I'd hope that I would be able to convince Daniel Jr. to come with me after all.

When I arrived at Carlos home, Daniel Jr. answered the door. I was so relieved to see him that I just grabbed him and hugged him!

"Ma, I am going to be alright," Daniel Jr. said.

"I will go to school and not get into any trouble."

"Please do not worry about me, ok."

"Daniel, I just cannot do this with you anymore. You are my son, and I love you. I want you with me, and I am so upset with you!"

"Ma, I am going to be 18 years old in two years. I know that Daniel Jr. and what?" I ask. What are your plans Daniel?"

"I don't know yet," Daniel replies. I just don't want to move to Daytona."

Mark had remained in the truck. Carlos had joined Mark as he waited for me.

"Sis, I got Daniel Jr." Carlos says walking back up to the house.

Carlos gave me a hug and kissed me on my cheek.

Go on and be happy Raquel," Carlos says.

Daniel Jr. mimics his uncle Carlos, gives me a hug, kisses me on my cheek, and says, "I love you mom, and I promise I will be fine."

"You promise?" I asked Daniel Jr. once more.

"I promise," Daniel Jr. replies. I hastily returned to the truck where Mark was waiting because I did not want Daniel Jr. to see me cry.

Mark also took me by my mother's house where my other three siblings were waiting to bid me farewell. I said goodbye to my mother, my sisters, Sashe and Selena, and another brother Eddie. My mother was concerned about me. She knew I had been through a lot and how upset I was about Daniel Jr. not coming with me, but she understood that I had to leave. She had also assured me that Carlos would take care of Daniel Jr. and for me not to worry about him.

CHAPTER THIRTY NINE

Mark and I finally arrived in Daytona, Florida. Wow! I could not believe I was finally here. I was ready to start a new life, get myself together, and live happily ever after! Daytona seemed quite different than Tampa. I was a little intrigued because I had never really lived anywhere else. Tampa was all I knew and wanted to forget. It was just refreshing for me to be in another domain, and I certainly embraced the thought of my future.

The ride to Daytona was exciting and melancholic for me at the same time. I was very excited about leaving; however, leaving Daniel Jr. behind was excruciating for me. I felt so guilty and helpless for leaving my baby. I didn't know what else I could have done! Was I a terrible mother for leaving my child like that? Did he know how much I love him? Did he know how sorry I was that he did not have the perfect family? I was sorry his father was not a part of his life like he should have been! That's all I ever wanted for Daniel Jr. I know that his dad loved him, but I could not make him love and stay with me. It was not Daniel Jr.'s fault. I wanted to provide a healthy, loving, stable environment for Daniel Jr. Sometimes things just don't work out the way we planned.

Mark and I pulled up to this modest, masonry, ranch style home. It was very nice, with a garage and satisfactory landscape. Mark drove the U-haul truck up into the driveway of the garage. He and Rachel had parked their own cars on the side of their home to reserve the space in garage driveway for the U-haul to be parked, and my car that was hitched on the back of the U-Haul.

I was really grateful to Mark and Rachel, because I knew they had made a lot of adjustments in their own lives to allow me to come and live with them for a while. I was also grateful to all of their encouragement and consolation for all that I had been through.

"You made it, girl," Rachel said excitingly as I made my way to her and Kassy, my ten-year-old neice.

"Hey, Auntie." Kassy followed.

We all embraced in a group hug.

"Yes, girl, I made it. Praise God," I replied with much relief.

"We are going to have some fun, girl. Mark and I are going to take you out this weekend," Rachel continued as we made our way into their home.

I was looking forward to going out and meeting some new people;

however, my main priorities were getting established, finding a job, getting into my own place, and getting Daniel Jr. here with me.

I felt like my life was doomed, and I did not understand why. There was no way I could remain in Tampa and I desired to get to another world. Initially, I had so many reservations. Daniel Jr. was definitely number one on my list.

CHAPTER FORTY

I had been in Daytona for about a month, found a job, and was moving into my own apartment in a couple of weeks! The transition here was a little challenging for me because I missed Daniel Jr. terribly, but I was learning my way around, and Mark and Rachel were wonderful.

I called to check on Daniel Jr. every day. Sometimes he was there to talk, and sometimes he was not.

"Carlos?"

"Yeah, sis. What's going on?"

"Not much."

"How is Daniel doing?"

"He's fine."

"Has he been going to school?"

"Yes, sis, he has been going to school," Carlos replied

"Is he staying out of trouble, Carlos?" I asked nervously.

"Yes, he has not been in any trouble," Carlos assures me.

Thank God! The last thing I wanted to hear was that Daniel Jr. had gotten into some more trouble or was not going to school.

"Carlos, I appreciate you so much looking out for him and allowing him to stay with you."

"I know you do, sis. Stop worrying about him so much!" Carlos demanded.

"Daniel Jr. is fine, and he is not a problem."

"Has he been eating right, Carlos?" I could not resist asking.

"Of course, sis! He eats what he wants. You know I like to eat, so he is eating whatever I eat," Carlos assured me.

"Okay, thanks Carlos. Tell my baby I love him and to please call me."

"I will."

I fought back tears as I hang up the phone.

Two weeks later, Carlos called to inform me that Daniel Jr. was arrested for selling marijuana! He was facing two years in prison! I was devastated!

CHAPTER FORTY ONE

Daniel Jr. was 16 years old and given two years in a minimum security prison. I went into a deep depression for a month. Mark and Rachel did everything they could to console and encourage me. I just did not want to be bothered with anyone and nothing!

I had moved into my own apartment and did not go anywhere but to work. I loved my new apartment, but it was hard for me to enjoy and embrace it because I was so sad about Daniel Jr.

Daniel Sr. had called me when he heard about Daniel Jr. I had not heard from Daniel Sr. in a year. I don't know how he got my number or knew I had left Tampa, but he found out somehow. I had stopped writing him after Clyde was killed.

"How ya doing Raquel?" Daniel Sr. sounded different. He almost sounded like a different person. It was hard to believe that Daniel Sr. had been in prison going on four years now!

I really was not in the mood to talk to him, but I did. Amazingly, Daniel Sr. was really cordial, and humble. He even expressed his condolences to me about Clyde!

"I know how much he meant to you, and I am sorry about his death," Daniel Sr. had said.

"Thank you Daniel," I replied.

"Raquel, you don't need to be sitting around there worrying about Daniel Jr.," Daniel Sr. said. Daniel Jr. made his choices, just like I did! Hopefully, with this little time he got, he will grow up, and stay his ass out of here!" Daniel Sr. said.

I could not cuss Daniel Sr. out because as much as I hate to admit it, he was right! But I did have some words for him!

"It is your fault, Daniel!" I yell. He is a duplicate of you! Had you been the father you should have been to him, he would not be there!"

"Raquel, it is not my fault Daniel Jr. was out there selling marijuana and got caught," Daniel angrily says. You are not going to put that guilt trip on me! I know I was not the daddy I should have been, but he made his own choices and you have to stop taking up for him!" I hate it that my son has ended up in the same place I am! It hurts me too, whether you believe it or not, but he made his own decision to do that! He surely did not have too, now did he?" Daniel Sr. says.

"Of course not," I finally reply.

"Ok then! I have to go now Raquel. I just wanted to call you to make sure you were ok and to tell you not to worry about Daniel Jr. He will be ok," Daniel Sr. concludes.

"Thank you Daniel," I replied.

"Take care of yourself Raquel," Daniel Sr. says and hangs up.

CHAPTER FORTY TWO

I had been in Daytona for eight months. Everything was going really well and I liked Daytona very much.

I had gone to see Daniel Jr. twice and was relieved that he was doing well and getting so big! He seemed to have matured a lot and was making plans for his future. Daniel Jr. was interested in music and singing, and he planned to pursue it as a career upon his release. I assured him I would do whatever I could to help him and that I loved him. He apologized for disappointing me and promised me he had learned his lesson. I could only continue to pray that he did.

Mark and Rachel had taken me out to a few clubs. It was refreshing to be out and socialize with new and different people.

Tommy and I met at a club one Friday night when Rachel and I decided to do a girl's night out, just the two of us. Mark stayed at home with Kassy, and allowed Rachel and I some time alone for bonding. He and Rachel seemed to have such a solid marriage. It was refreshing and encouraging to me to see how they loved, cared, trusted, and respected each other.

As Rachel and I entered the club, we were immediately met with stares and glances from both men and women. We were used to attention because we were identical twins, and we looked good! Rachel and I were in our thirties and wore it well. We had been to this club a couple of other times, and Mark had been our escort. I enjoyed myself both times, but I had a feeling I was going to have a fabulous time tonight!

I had on a pair of black dress slacks and a cute little black halter blouse. I had lost about ten pounds since my transition to Daytona, worrying about Daniel Jr.; however, I was pleased about my weight loss, and had hoped to maintain it. Rachel looked very nice in her black and white dress.

Immediately upon entering the club, Rachel and I spotted an empty table in the rear of the room, adjacent to the bar.

"Rachel, there is a table in the back, next to the bar." I pointed.

Rachel really preferred to sit in the front area. I preferred that as well, but the place was so packed that there were only a few tables left in the rear of club. Rachel glanced around to ensure there were no more tables available in the front, while I assured her the same.

We headed to the rear of the club, and I noticed several guys "checking us out," as we made our way to claim our table. Of course, some of the women were staring and rolling their eyes. Haters, no doubt! Rachel and I surely paid no attention to that. In fact, we were used to that too.

When we made it to our table, a couple of guys were standing "guard" near our chairs. They pretended to be engaged in conversation with each other, but I sensed their topic of discussion was Rachel and I. I noticed one of the guys immediately, because his cologne captivated me. He was also well dressed, clean-shaven with an immaculate haircut, and quite attractive. He was holding a glass in one hand, and graciously stepped back away from the chair I was headed to, and extended it for my seating. His friend who was standing there with him was not bad looking either. He reminded me somewhat of the *R&B singer, Keith Sweat.* He extended Rachel's chair for her to sit.

Rachel and I had settled comfortably at our table and summons the waitress for cocktails. The waitress made her way to Rachel and I, and took our drink orders. As the waitress exited our table, the guy whom I had noticed upon Rachel and I entrance made his way to our table.

"How are y'all doing?"

"We are fine," I replied confidently.

"Where are ya'll from?"

Rachel re-positioned herself in her seat. Her gesture implied that she was somewhat intrigued with this guy's intrusion.

"I moved here from Tampa, Florida almost two years now," Rachel replied. "My sister, Raquel, moved here almost a year ago."

I knew Rachel must have approved of him somewhat, because she would have never offered him any explanation for anything. I, on the other hand, had been through so much with no good men that I had become cynical. I simply had no patience for any shit from any of them. I still had faith that I would meet Mr. Right and get married someday; however, I did not have time for their lame ass stories and excuses. It was all about me now!

"So, what is your name?" Rachel asks. "Tommy Davis" he replied.

"And your friend?" I ask.

"Oh, that's Kevin Lang," Tommy answers.

Tommy appeared to be doing pretty well for himself. He definitely smelled damn good, and seemed to have good taste. He was well groomed and sharp. He had on a nice bone color linen shirt and matching pants. His caramel colored shoes appeared to be genuine snakeskin and complemented his attire perfectly. He also flashed some nice gold jewelry: a herringbone necklace and Gucci bracelet and watch. I did not see a wedding band, and I was very pleased about that.

"What are ya'll drinking'?" Tommy finally asked just as our waitress was returning with our drinks.

"I am drinking Brandy and Coke, and my sister is drinking an Apple Martini." I reply. "Will you be taking care of this tab?" I ask Tommy.

"Sure, I got yall," Tommy replies with no hesitation. The waitress gives her nod of approval as Tommy reached in his pocket and handed her a $50 bill.

Now that's what I'm talking about, a sponsor. I liked Tommy already. If there was one thing I despised, that was a cheap man. If they were not spending any money and buying drinks, I did not tolerate them in my face.

Tommy finished his drink after paying the waitress and then disappeared. I wondered if he was for real or just perpetrating. As I was looking around the club, absorbing the scene, I noticed that Tommy had rejoined his friend Kevin at the bar. They were laughing and seem to be having a good time. Cockishly, Kevin made his way over to us at our table with a partial drink in hand. I guess, he and Tommy were a tag team.

"So, ya'll just moved here from Tampa?" he asked.

Rachel gave him a look as if she was irritated, and then glanced at me to ensure that I had this. I had a whole new attitude about men. I was not cutting them any slack. I was not tolerating any questioning or sweating me, unless he was being gracious and attentive to my needs and desires. I simply had no time for the interrogations, and I was not interested in what their zodiac sign was. Furthermore, I had no problem telling them that.

"And you are?" I asked a bit sarcastically, although Tommy had already told us his friend's name.

"Oh, I'm sorry. I am Kevin," he replied.

I decided to cut him some slack since he was Tommy's friend, and he did pretty much secure a table for Rachel and me. But, if he was going to contemplate being in my face for the duration, he damn sure had better been spending some money; otherwise, he would have to re-locate. And I meant that!

Tommy returned to the table where Rachel and I were, and a waitress was accompanying him. "Tell her what ya'll are drinking," Tommy solicited confidently.

"I will have another Brandy on the rocks with a splash of Coke," I replied with a bit of attitude.

I could see Tommy checking me out as he sipped on his drink.

"I will have an Apple Martini," Rachel followed modestly.

The waitress made notation on her pad studiously.

"Kevin, what are you having, man?" Tommy asked.

Kevin had attempted to make small conversation with Rachel and me for a few minutes, before Tommy's re-appearing. He was primarily focused on Rachel, but of course Rachel displayed no interest in him, so he finally resigned back "on guard" and allowed Tommy to continue to make his case.

"Just give me a Hennessey and Coke," Kevin replied happily.

I could tell Kevin's ass was cheap! He was all right looking and appeared to be cool, but I could spot cheap anywhere, and his ass was cheap. The waitress glanced at Tommy for his nod of approval, which he gave confidently.

"Bring me another one, too," Tommy concluded as the waitress nodded and summed up the tab from our table.

"Will that be all, Tommy?" the waitress inquired of Tommy.

"Yeah, baby, that's it. Thank you," Tommy responded rather graciously.

Tommy helped himself to a vacant seat next to mine.

"Thank you for the drinks," I initiated.

"Oh, you are quite welcome," Tommy responded "So you two are sisters?"

"Yes, we are identical twins," I answered.

Rachel smiled somewhat approvingly at Tommy and I dialogue.

"Yes, I can see you two are twins," Tommy replies.

"Which one of ya'll is the oldest?"

"I am," I replied.

"So you just moved here?" He asked.

"Yes, about eight months ago," I replied.

"So what brought you here to Daytona?" he asked.

"I just wanted a fresh start," I answered casually, not to solicit any further information unless it was necessary.

"Are you running from something or someone?" Tommy boldly inquired.

"No, not necessarily," I replied.

Rachel was undoubtedly analyzing the conversation mentally.

"Where is your husband or your man?" Tommy asks.

"Where is your wife or girlfriend," Rachel intercepted.

"Oh, I am not married, baby. I am single," Tommy replied.

"Oh, so you don't have a woman then?" Rachel continued to drill Tommy.

"I have friends, but I am not committed to anyone right now."

"Oh, you have friends?" Rachel asked.

"Yes, friends," Tommy affirmed.

"Hey, Tommy," a couple of women intruded.

"Oh, hey, Simone and Claire." Tommy stood up to greet them graciously.

Both were nice looking women, very well dressed in chic pantsuits.

"Raquel," Tommy directed his attention back to me. "These are two friends of mine. Simone, Claire, this is Raquel and her twin sister Rachel," he introduces the women to us.

"Hi," I replied, repositioning myself in my chair confidently.

Rachel offered no sentiments. She was skeptical about *any* woman and did not befriend them easily. The two of us only had a few mutual friends, whom we actually claimed as our "sisters" because we had been friends since grade school. They were the only women that Rachel really embraced. She just didn't trust women. She felt like all they wanted to do was get in one's business. I enjoyed the challenge with woman. I was competitive and confident of myself, no matter what I'd been through with no good ass men.

Simone was very attractive. She seemed to be in her mid or late thirties. She had a nice cocoa complexion, sported a chic white pantsuit, gold shoes, accessories, and a gold beaded handbag. Her hair was shoulder length and draped as if it had been wrapped. She seemed to have attitude. I could appreciate that, because she reminded me of myself somewhat.

Claire was very attractive, too. She appeared to be in her mid to late thirties as well. She had a smooth creamy complexion light-skinned like Rachel and I. Claire sported a navy blue pantsuit, silver shoes and accessories, and a silver clutch-style bag. Her hair was shoulder length as well, but it was locked in curls that complimented her cute round face almost flawlessly.

I could tell that "Ms. Simone" was perhaps the lead, and the one who was interested in Tommy. She sort of gave a reluctant "hello" when Tommy introduced us to her, all the while staring me down from head to toe.

Claire seemed a little more personable. She did offer a moderate "hello" and to my surprise, she extended her hand to Rachel and I as she greeted us. Simone, seemed to be annoyed at Claire's graciousness towards Raquel and I, because she revealed a hideous grin.

Thank God, the waitress appeared with our drinks. She placed our drinks on the table in front of Rachel and I, and handed us cocktail napkins. She then handed Tommy and Kevin their drinks.

Tommy, who had still been engaged in conversation with Simone and Claire, excused himself to go take care of the tab. Prior to leaving to go take care of the tab, Tommy turned to me to ensure that I was o.k.

"Raquel, are you cool?"

"Sure. Thank you for the drinks," I replied.

"No problem," Tommy replied.

Tommy then turned to Simone and Claire to inquire what their choice of drinks were.

"I'll have a glass of Chardonnay," Simone said.

"Claire, what are your drinking?" Tommy asked.

"Uh, just get me gin and tonic with a twist of lime," Claire replied.

Tommy then turned to the waitress, who was already writing down the women's requests. She nodded at Tommy to let him know that she had their orders and left to retrieve Simone and Claire's drinks.

Tommy continued chatting with Simone and Claire until the waitress returned with their drinks. She handed both ladies their drinks and asked Tommy if he needed anything else.

"No, that's it for now, baby. Thank you," Tommy replied appreciatively.

"Well, it was good seeing ya'll, Simone, Claire." I heard Tommy say to the two *intruders*.

Simone appeared annoyed at Tommy; obviously because he was bidding she and Claire farewell and anxious to return to entertain some *real divas!*

"Oh, you are leaving?" Simone inquired of Tommy, snobbishly.

Here we go.. Tommy was obviously *dealing* with Simone. Tommy gave Simone an annoyed look.

"Yes, I am going back to my seat," he said.

There was a pause between Simone and Tommy both for a minute, and Simone seemed to be thinking, *"No, he didn't!"*

Yes, he did, bitch, I thought with a smirk on my face.

Simone then seductively took another sip of her drink and summoned Claire.

"Let's go."

Simone glanced at me one more time, then turned to walk away. Claire "followed the leader". Tommy turned away and headed back to Rachel and I table.

CHAPTER FORTY THREE

Tommy and I dated for a year before he proposed to me. Tommy's controlling, jealous, insecure, abusive, narcissistic ways were a presage to just what I had to look forward to, and I should have taken heed to them, but instead I agreed to marry him. I was thirty-two years old, and had wanted to get married for so long. I believed that Tommy loved me, and would change.

When I first met Tommy, I was attracted to his style, his class, and his confidence. He always dressed so nice, and neat, and always smelled so good. Tommy was very conscientious about his appearance, and wore only the best. I had loved that about him, too.

Tommy also had extremely extravagant taste. Everyone would always compliment him on his appearance, or how good he smelled.

Tommy exposed me to things no man had ever done, and had made me feel special, desired, and needed. Tommy took me everywhere he went, if I so desired.

I received a lot of gifts from Tommy and, we frequently dined out, and indulged in a lot of entertainment. We did everything together, *and* he was great in bed!

Tommy always got me a present and card on all holidays... Easter, Valentines, Birthday, Anniversary ... and he never forgot, never. Even if we were angry at each other, Tommy always took care of me, and I most definitely took care of him.

Tommy was the only man who ever took me on *real* vacations. We went to Las Vegas every year, sometimes twice. He loved to party and go out, and he always wanted me with him. I did not like to go out all of the time, so Tommy would sometimes go alone or with friends. I had no problem with that, because I trusted him completely in that capacity.

Tommy was also very attentive to me when I was sick, or not feeling well. He worked everyday *like a man should,* and took care of all of his responsibilities of taking care of his share of bills, and our home.

Tommy was a faithful husband; that is, I never had to deal with other women. He was not a cheater. He took care of our home and me. We took vacations every year, partied together, shopped together, but inside of me, deep inside, I was a mess! I felt like a prisoner, so trapped, with absolutely no way out! *Tommy was a faithful husband, so how in the hell, or why in the hell would I leave him?*

That was my ultimate struggle, and what kept me in the marriage for as long as I was. I also loved Tommy's family dearly. But I was always depressed, crying, so unhappy, and never wanted to do anything or go anywhere.

Tommy **also** had a terrible temper. He was extremely jealous, insecure, cruel, disrespectful, and controlling. It caused so many problems in our marriage. Although, I never had to worry about him cheating on me, which is one of the reasons I sustained a momentous of respect for him and held on to my marriage with everything I had.

Tommy did not want me socializing with anyone. He was so jealous of my son, Daniel Jr. which caused terrible turmoil in our marriage, with me fighting him so desperately on that saga. He did not like any of my friends and would embarrass me badly in front of them, and my family. Tommy had this notion that he was the reason that I had what I had: a nice home, car, and a decent job. He never would accept the fact that I had all of that before I met him, or that I had a life before him!

Tommy was also abusive to me both physically and emotionally. He was always fussing, cursing, criticizing, disrespecting me, and anyone who knew me, or thought they knew me. He was obnoxious in private, but his best performances were of course in public. Tommy would disrespect me in front of family and friends, and save his "grand finales" to perform in front of my son. It was terrible. He was so jealous of my son, and my son hated him too. Imagine living in the middle of that! My son's hatred of Tommy stemmed from his witness of how Tommy disrespected me.

Tommy was so disturbed. I had never met anyone like him. We all have issues, but Tommy's issues literally drained me dry! God knows I tried to sustain my marriage, until I just gave up the ghost and lost all will to fight for it anymore.

Tommy had sucked the life out of me with his nonsense, and no matter how many times I attempted to talk to him and reason with him, he just did not get it, or just did not want to get it! He just did not give a damn what anyone said or felt; he was always right, and everyone else was crazy, not him! It was insane; he'd made me insane! After five years of marriage, I finally had to accept the fact that something was very wrong with Tommy; mentally, emotionally, physically, I don't know, but I realized that I could not fix it. I really wish I could have, but I couldn't!

I did everything to maintain my marriage to no avail. It was such a struggle for such a long time. Ultimately, Tommy had just drained me where I had nothing else to give. I literally felt like dying. I was surely dead emotionally.

I begged Tommy for years and tried to talk to him so many times, but he just would not get it! I had left him several times, and eventually returned to him; although, nothing had ever changed with him or the marriage in itself.

Eventually, over the years, he pretended to be better, after me leaving him twice, and finally putting my foot down on so many things, but he had already damaged me emotionally. I was already scarred emotionally when I met him, from my previous relationship with Daniel Sr., and Tommy just affected me more.

Of course, when we would talk about it, and I would tell him how I felt, his response was always, "You act like I am the worst man you ever had."

I would re-assure him by saying, "Absolutely not. In fact, you are the best, *but* some things about you, Tommy..."

I fought so hard for my marriage. I did a lot of praying, fasting, crying, yelling, cursing, everything, and ultimately, the struggle just drained me emotionally and physically.

Tommy was a good husband and provider *in some ways*, and because of that it scared me to death just the thought of losing him. I did not think I could ever find anyone as faithful as Tommy, but his controlling, obnoxious, intimidating, disrespectful, insecure issues had shut me down. His attitude had affected me badly emotionally whereas I had no desire to have sex with him. I was always a sensual woman, but my libido had ceased, and this was a huge problem for me.

Even when Tommy and I were doing great and I was feeling good, at least on the surface, I still could not acquire the desire for sex with my husband, and that affected me even more emotionally. Tommy accepted it and dealt with it. He never pressured me, and I felt so bad about not being able to have sex with my husband! I did express this to him. I also tried to talk to him so many times about "our lack of intimacy", and what the cause was, but I don't think he ever got it. He just pretended as if nothing was wrong.

I think he fully understood what he had done to me and what he was doing to me, but he would not accept the responsibility of how he failed our marriage and me. He did not want to change and always wanted to be in control.

I truly loved my husband, at one time, but he destroyed the passion and yearning I had for him. I was no longer *in* love with him. I had to face the fact that something was truly lost between us, and it killed me to suffer, and to see *him* suffering, too.

We had no marriage. It was no life for either of us, but we continued on in our relationship. For the most part, we were just "comfortable", and we had settled in this marriage. We were just "used to each other".

Tommy and I both did not want to give up all that each of us had invested into the marriage, although ultimately I did.

So, because of my vulnerability, brokenness, stupidity, and un-resolved feelings, I allowed myself to be victimized again by Daniel Sr. after he was released from prison. Yeah, one would have thought I had learned my lesson from my past with him. I truly thought that I was over him, and that there was no way I would ever allow him to hurt me again, ever in life.

I knew not to believe Daniel Sr. claiming that "he loved me, he had grown up, and we were going to be together again and have a good life together." I knew that Daniel Sr. was never up to any good! I was vulnerable because of a miserable and unhappy marriage, and so drained emotionally that I simply had no fight.

So I was unable to "resist the devil and flee." I succumbed to Daniel Sr.'s schemes and temptations.

I stood on that mountain and believed that I could have the whole world with Daniel Sr. finally. I wanted to believe that he had really changed, matured, and wanted us to "start over." So, I plunged over the mountain, and that was it. *I gave up my soul to the Devil!*

CHAPTER FORTY FOUR

If it was one thing he did not tolerate, it was cheating. Tommy never cheated on me. Women and men both used to come to me and tell me how committed he was to me. Tommy would tell anyone quick, "I am married, and I love my wife."

But I was so miserable, for so long.

I did love Tommy initially, but towards the conclusion of such a tumultuous marriage with him, my passion for him seemed to have been excavated due to his emotional and physical abuse towards me.

Daniel Sr. and I had talked on the phone a few times when he got out of prison. Of course it was in secret, because Tommy was so jealous, and he hated the mere name of Daniel Sr.

I know if things had been better between Tommy and me, I would have never stooped as low as I did and allowed myself to be manipulated by Daniel Sr. again.

Daniel Sr. used me, and I will never forgive myself for allowing him to do that to me again. As for Daniel Sr., what can I say other than he must pay? I don't blame anyone except myself for the worst mistake I'd ever made in my life; I knew better.

Even though I had gone on with my life, and married Tommy, unfortunately, it was a horrific marriage that would not last. After serving ten years in prison, Daniel Sr. was released. I let him do it to me again, and this was the worst ever. He contacted me when he was released and said he wanted to see me. I was so vulnerable at this time, so I gave in.

Daniel Sr. and I met secretly for a couple of months, meeting at hotels. He had convinced me that "we were going to be together." So, when Daniel Sr. asked me for money "to help him get a place to stay and some other necessities he needed," I believed him like a fool, and gave him some money. I was excited about the "future" Daniel Sr. was planning for us, and I was planning my escape from my hellish marriage.

After Daniel Sr. took advantage of my state of being and my unresolved feelings for him, he got what he wanted from me, and simply gave me his ass to kiss. It killed me inside; I mean it was really the worst state I had been in emotionally. *How could I have trusted him, believed in him, gave him my money, gave him my body, gave him my love? I sacrificed everything for him like a fool, and when I lost it, his response to me was,* "Man, that's your problem; you should have never got married." He played me like a "real sucker", as he would say, and I foolishly went for it.

I had no one to blame but myself, because I knew better. I knew not to trust him, or fall for his lies and promises again.

Once Daniel Sr. got the money from me, I did not hear from him again. I tried to call him several times, but he had changed his number. I had no other way to contact him and knew nothing about where he was. I was crushed and felt so stupid! Of all the thirty-seven years of my life, I had never hurt so badly. It was pure torture. I had never been so humiliated, and felt so used in my life. I could not blame anyone but myself; I was reaping what I sowed, too. *This* changed me forever.

CHAPTER FORTY FIVE

Things were no better between Tommy and I, and I made a conscientious decision and told Tommy about Daniel Sr. and I "affair."

Consciously, I think I confessed also because it was a sure way of escape for me out of a miserable, life-sucking marriage. I was embarrassed to do so, and I knew Tommy would not tolerate my indiscretion, but I had to relieve myself of the burden. It was too much for me, and this life-sucking marriage I was in, was too much for me, too! I wanted out of this freaking prison!

I told Tommy that I had loved him in the beginning, but he had destroyed my love for him at the end. I was no longer *in* love with him but I did care about what happened to him. I wanted the best for him, and I did not want him to hurt anymore. But, he had depleted me, rather than complete me.

Ultimately, I just lost my mind and succumbed to my past, which debilitated me even more. I knew I had disappointed him, and hurt him badly, but I was hurting, too! I could not keep the truth about what I allowed to happen between Daniel Sr. and I anymore.

I would always have Tommy's best interest at heart. I pitied him for the way he was, and I really wanted all to be well and work out for him.

I left Tommy for the third time, and that was it for me. I had no desire to return to the relationship under any circumstances. And I didn't!

CHAPTER FORTY SIX

I filed for a divorce from Tommy about a year after our separation. I was so relieved when he finally signed the papers and granted me my freedom. I relinquished my home and everything in it, except the clothes on back all to Tommy to ensure a civil, peaceful dissolution of the marriage.

A couple of months after Tommy and I divorce was finalized, I had purchased five lottery tickets on a whim. Amazingly, one of my tickets matched all six numbers in the Florida Lottery. I could not believe it! I had won one hundred twenty seven million dollars after taxes becoming an instant multi millionaire!

I thought about Tommy often. *How was he doing? Was he finally happy? Had he forgiven me?* I'd hoped his heart had healed about us and about life itself.

I was not obliged to give Tommy anything; however, after I had confirmed that I had actually won, and secured me an attorney, I called and told him.

"Hi, Tommy, this is Raquel."

"Mmmm, how you doing, Raquel?" he asked, trying to sound "okay," which I knew he was not. Tommy hated losing me. I was the best woman he'd ever had, but he messed up. I knew he missed me, and I did miss him in some ways, but I had no desire to go back.

I wanted Tommy to be happy, and all to be well with him always. I had not talked to Tommy, nor had I seen him since the divorce. I did my best not to run into him or go anywhere where I thought he would be. I did not want to see his pain, and I did not want to regress to my own.

"I'm fine," I casually replied, trying not to burst. "How have you been, Tommy? How is Momma?"

"Momma" was Tommy's mother, whom would always be my mother-in-law. She was the best, and Tommy was so blessed to have her as a mother.

"I'm doing fine, and momma is doing okay."

"Good," I replied. "So are you still working hard?" I ask.

"Yeah, I got to pay my bills." Tommy replied.

"Yeah, don't we all?"

"So what drop shot are you seeing?" Nobody I know, I hope." Tommy inquires.

He'll never change. Thank God I no longer have to hear this nonsense.

"Tommy," I replied, not even responding to his undying sarcasm. "You can quit your job."

"Why? Are you going to give me some money? Did you hit the lottery or something?"

Little does he know, as a matter of fact, I did!

"As a matter of fact I did," I replied.

"What, Raquel? Are you kidding me? You hit that one hundred seventy five million?" Tommy asks in astonishment.

"It was one hundred twenty seven million after taxes; I opted to have the cash up front."

"Damn, Raquel!" *Damn!*" Tommy screamed.

"Tommy," I said calmly, not trying to lead him on about us, or anything else. "I need your bank account number; I am wiring you five million dollars."

"What?" Tommy replied.

Tommy was speechless for once in his life.

"I can't believe this; you're joking me, right?"

"No, I am serious, Tommy. You never have to work a day in your life again, as long as you don't squander it. I know that you are responsible and will take care of yourself."

"Thanks, Raquel, thank you," Tommy responded emotionally.

"Raquel, I am sorry for the things I did to you, and how I hurt you. I realize now that I had issues."

"Tommy, I know. I am sorry, too, but I am happier now... even more so now. I just want the best for you as well."

I knew Tommy was sorry, but was just too damn prideful to admit that he had issues.

"We had our time together, and it did not work, Tommy; you know that, and I know that," I say.

"I know, Raquel. Well, don't give all your money to those drop shots."

I ignored this response again. Tommy swears I left him for another man. I stopped trying to convince him that I did not, a long time ago.

"Tommy, I am putting an additional one and a half million dollars into your account to be given as follows." I read off a list that I had compiled.

- Dean and Sally (Tommy's brother and wife) $250,000
- Susan (Tommy's niece) $250,000
- Tracy (Tommy's niece) $250,000
- Dean, Jr. (Tommy's nephew) $100,000
- Toby (Tommy's son) $100,000

- Momma (Tommy's mother) $100,000
- Auntie Claire (Tommy's mother's sister) $100,000
- Aunt Rena (Tommy's aunt) $50,000
- Jack and Rita (Tommy's uncle and wife) $50,000
- Junior (Tommy's older brother) $50,000
- Karen (Tommy's sister) $25,000
- Sojourne (Tommy's sister) $25,000
- Mally (Tommy's sister) $25,000
- Henry (Tommy's brother) $25,000
- Joel (Tommy's brother) $25,000
- Cecilia (Tommy knows who she is) $25,000
- Barry and Macy (Tommy's friends) $50,000
- Tommy $5,000,000

"The total is six million, five hundred thousand dollars." I affirm.

"What? Raquel, that is nice of you. I know you always loved my family, and they you. They still ask about you," Tommy says.

"Please let them know that I am fine, and I will always love them."

"Tommy, I trust you to give the money to everyone as I have asked of you. I am leaving you in charge of that, but expect each person I've outlined to receive their money. The only stipulation that they won't, would be if something happens to them, God forbid, and then it will go to you; their share, that is. I am having my attorney to draw up papers for you to sign ordering that, okay?"

"Yes, Raquel. You know I appreciate it, and I will give them their share."

"All right, the money will be wired tomorrow morning. My attorney will be calling you to have you come down and sign the documents before the money is available for you to receive."

"Raquel, thank you, and I really appreciate you."

"I know, Tommy," I quickly reply.

"I have to go."

"Take care of yourself."

"Don't party too hard, and don't give all of your money to the "gold diggers," I laughed, giving him a dose of his own insanity. "And Tommy, take care of yourself," I conclude and hang up the phone.

Tommy and I failure in marriage was in no way due to my adulterous act, because our marriage was over long before I plunged into that hell hole, I would always care about Tommy. He failed me, and I had failed him, too. So, I had vowed to myself that if he had ever needed anything, and I had it, he would get it.

CHAPTER FORTY SEVEN

A year had gone by, since I had won 127 million dollars in the Florida lottery. I was rich, single, and pursuing many of my dreams.

I had finally finished my studies in Creative Arts, received my Masters degree, and I was working for myself creating advertisement portfolios for some commercial businesses.

I was also making various financial investments all over the world to ensure wise dividends and provisions for Daniel Jr. and my family. I was very responsible with my lottery winnings and was not going to just squander it all away. This time, I was in control of Raquel! Finally, I felt better about myself and loved me. And it was not just about me winning millions, but that surely helped!

I was also in a fulfilling relationship, and more importantly, happy and content after 40 years of misery!

Daniel Jr. had been home now for three years and was doing really well. He had got married to his high school sweetheart and they had blessed me with my beautiful grandson Daniel West III.

I had relocated to the fabulous South Beaches of Miami from Daytona, Florida and purchased my dream home. It was a red brick Spanish Villa home on South Miami Beach. It consisted of six bedrooms, four full baths, and one master bedroom with bathroom. I had it decorated by professional interior decorators with *my* emphasis of décor and design. I simply loved it!

One of the rooms I had decorated especially for my grandson, Daniel III, whom was two years old now. My home was not his domicile, but I wanted to ensure he always had his own special room whenever he would visit me. I was really crazy about that child. I had also secured a trust fund for him to attend college, and I had also made provisions for him once he graduated from college.

I also purchased my mother a new home, in Tampa Florida where she and my family still resided. My siblings and I were very close, and I certainly made sure they were taken care of too. I had set my sisters and brothers up with new homes, cars, and plenty of money in their bank accounts.

Daniel Jr. was fulfilling his dream embarking on a professional singing career. I got him affiliated with some people in the music industry, and invested a lot of money into him. My only mandate was that his father would *not* be involved with his success and future prosperity.

Daniel Jr. and his father apparently had been in contact with each other after Daniel Jr. was released from prison. He had told me that his dad wanted to get in touch with me so that he and I could talk.

I had never tried to sway Daniel Jr.'s feelings about his dad, and my intentions were not to interfere with their relationship. My only vow was that he was not going to take advantage of my son like he had done to me! I was making it *my* business to manage and help facilitate Daniel Jr.'s career and all monetary and legal decisions had to go through me first! His slick talking, manipulating, father was not going to take advantage of my son like he had done to me.

CHAPTER FORTY EIGHT

Daniel Sr. had finally tracked me down through our son, Daniel Jr.

He and I had spoken on the phone a few occasions and it was just "small talk". Of course, he had the audacity to call me, just like I knew he would eventually after he'd learned about me hitting the lottery and re-locating to Miami.

"How ya' doing, Raquel?" His usual shallow greeting, like he really gave a damn!

"I'm great, of course, Daniel," I replied subtlety.

"Yeah, I guess you are with all of that money," he replied.

"You are correct again, Daniel, as you always were," I respond sarcastically.

"What do you mean by that?" Daniel Sr. responded.

I re-positioned myself in my red marble Victorian sauna, as I sipped my delightful glass of Moet champagne preparing to respond, because I didn't intend to go back to *Wonderland* with this miserable legion. I totally ignored his silly question, and decided to relieve him of some of his misery.

"Raquel, I'm here in Miami right now, and I would love to see you."

"Really?" I replied. "Well, you may be in luck, Daniel. So why don't we have dinner, Daniel, and perhaps some dessert for old times sake?"

"Yeah, I'd like that, Raquel."

I bet you would.

After crushing whatever piece of heart I had left, this scum-sucking leech had the audacity to call me gloating for some of my money, no doubt.

"Mmm, that sounds intriguing to me, Daniel," I replied.

"Yeah, I know no one has given it to you like daddy will."

If only he knew! Yeah, he *was* the best, even though he didn't last long, but he *was* very effective.

"I can't believe you hit that lottery, Raquel! I've been trying to hit it so that I can come and get you," Daniel Sr. lied. "So, Raquel, I know I am good for something!" Daniel confidently claims.

"You bet, baby; you know I got you covered."

Yeah, you are good for something alright! A burial! And I am going to make sure you get it!

Stupid bastard! He thought he was so smart, and so cool, and so fine, and his sex was so good, even though he never lasted more than five minute, but he did know how to "swallow a woman up" as his no good ass would say. Although I loved it, I could probably live without it. *Nah, just kidding!* I loved to feel my man *in* me, but I had no problem with Daniel Sr. "swallowing me up" because of all of the sexual diseases he had given me, I'd hoped that he would catch them and deteriorate, and ultimately go to Hell!

"Okay, Daniel, when do you want to do this?" I asked.

"Tonight, Raquel," he said.

Right answer, Mr. Blake! "Great, I'll have a limo pick you up. Where should we pick you up at?"

The gutter?

"A limousine?" he stupidly asked. "Are you coming with him?"

"Of course, Daniel, I will be accompanying him," I assured him.

"Mmm, let me think," Daniel Sr. replied. "Have him pick me up on Carter Street, in front of that pink building. I'll be standing outside."

"Sure, Daniel, what time?"

"Let me see... at 8:00 sharp."

"No problem, Daniel. My driver will be there at 8:00 sharp."

"Did you want me to stay all night?"

But of course, your ass won't be leaving. "That would be nice. Do you think you could pull it off?" I said.

"I dunno, but I'll think of somethin'. "Shit, with all of that money you got, I don't care what the bitch (his girl, Leslie) thinks."

Daniel Sr. was such a low-life. I was not surprised that he and Leslie were still together.

"Fine, Daniel; we'll see you then, okay?"

"Okay, Raquel, love ya."

I bet you do.

"I will see you later, Daniel," and I conclude the conversation.

Okay, Raquel, this is it! He has to pay for what he did to me. I cannot think or feel anything else. I was totally numb, and he did this to me! I was always a loving, caring person. I never tried to hurt anyone. But *he* made me hate! And I do hate him! He was an egotistical, despicable male species. I wanted him to suffer like I suffered for twenty-five years, which commenced when I first met him!

I am not angry any more with him for not loving me, or leaving me for another woman; I really am not. I realize that he was not part of the *divine plan* for my future.

What infuriated me was the way he took advantage of me when he was released from prison. Not to mention the emotional trauma, and pain that never ceased, after he just walked out of my life with no regard for his son or me!

My heart was shattered, but I had to go on for Daniel Jr.'s sake. I felt rejected, worthless, unloved, and unwanted. I had given this man ten years of my life, and gave birth to his first child. I was devoted to Daniel Sr. and his treatment to me was without merit.

Wow! This all seems surreal! I still cannot believe that I actually won the lottery, and finally I get my sweet revenge on Daniel Sr. Forgive me, Lord. I am sorry, but this time, revenge is Raquel's.

CHAPTER FORTY NINE

It had been a couple of years since I saw Daniel Sr. last.

"I had heard you hit the lottery; you look good, too, Raquel!" .

"I was not going to bother you, though. I already took you through enough. I did not want you to think I wanted anything from you," Daniel Sr. said.

For a moment, he had almost convinced me that he was actually sincere. *Slick Bastard!*

"You know, Raquel, one thing about you is, that you always had class. You always had your shit together, and I mean that. My pride just never allowed me to tell you that. The way I treated you, and let you go, I was a damn fool." Daniel Sr. says.

Well, for once in his life, he was telling the truth.

"I always loved you Raquel. I know you do not believe that, but God knows.

Wow, I wish I had a camera; this was really a Kodak moment.

"Damn, Raquel, you look so damn sweet!"

"Sweet enough to eat?" I teased.

I was *not* teasing! Daniel Sr. will get one final chance to do just that. His eyes gazed into mine, and I welcomed his gaze deceitfully. I remained poised and in control of myself, especially my heart.

I knew I was looking good. I was wearing a camel color Michael Kohr strapless silk dress, which consoled my perfect size nine figure beautifully. My Michael Kohr six-inch heels accentuated my sensuality, exuberant confidence and total control. My hair was freshly done in micro braids, which undoubtedly took ten years off of my maturity.

"Wow, Raquel, you really look good,"" Daniel, Sr. acknowledged again. "I mean real good! I can see you really been taking care of yourself." Daniel Sr. continued to give me my due props.

"Thank you, Daniel," I replied confidently. "You look pretty good yourself." I decided to give him his props, too.

Daniel Sr. was a good-looking man, and well groomed. He still had his youthful face and body. He was dressed nicely, smelling good and fresh haircut. He was wearing a nice, immaculate creased pair of designer jeans, a white oxford shirt, and some black Italian loafers. His cologne was a little intimidating for me, because I really loved for a man to smell good. That just really turned me on. But, I maintained my composure, and kept my mind on my *last laugh!*

CHAPTER FIFTY

Whenever Daniel Sr. came around me, I used to totally come undone, but *finally*, I was together in every way. I had loved Daniel, Sr. like no other man in my life, ever, and truly had given up all hope of ever loving like that again. In fact, I did not want to love a man the way I had lost myself in Daniel Sr. That was such an unhealthy love; but I did want to be in love and to be loved in the same manner. I wanted that more than anything in life, even hitting the lottery! Now I have both, my man who truly loves me back, and all the money I'll ever need!

Daniel, Sr. had broken me. He had hurt me so bad, and left an indelible scar in my soul. I could not think of any good thing he had ever done to me or for me in the twenty-eight years of me knowing him. He had treated me so bad when we were together, yet I remained faithful.

I was so young and in love. I will never understand why and how I could love someone, who would cause me so much pain. I remember *no* happiness with Daniel Sr., only tears and total brokenness. He had no conscience when it came to me. He did not care about the pain and agony he had inflicted upon me. All he cared about was himself, getting money, and screwing around with women. He treated his other women like gold. But *me*, he defiled! I had given birth to his first son, whom was a duplicate of him, unfortunately; nevertheless, I got no esteem for that from Daniel Sr. I was, and still am, a good person. Of all of the men in the world, my life was doomed when I met him. I continued to make wrong choices with men. Daniel Sr. did me in, but let's sees who gets the *last laugh!*

"So, Raquel, you got it going on now, huh?" Daniel Sr. asks.

"Always did; you were just not capable of handling that, ever," I replied.

"What do you mean, Raquel? I was a player. "I was a young man." I stopped him right there. "Baby, this is the end. It is what it is. Yesterday is gone." "You made your choices Daniel, and "I did what I had to do."

"It does not matter now. I loved you; always did, always will. That's why you are here, right?" I ask.

"Right," he said. "And I loved you! I'm still in love with you, Raquel" Daniel Sr. claimed.

"Mmm hmm. I just want to spend the evening with you. We make each other feel good. No strings attached. I go on my way, and you go on back to your family. Oh, I also have a surprise to give you."

Boy, do I have a surprise for his ass!

"I want nothing more," I explained. "No relationship, no nothing. You don't have to worry about me calling you, or your people, as you always accused me of, and there would be no need for you to do likewise. I've accepted all things, but most of all, I've accepted there will never be you and me again," I concluded.

Daniel Sr. stared at me like he wanted to say something, but dared not to.

Our dialogue ceased just as my limo driver pulled into this illustrious grand hotel. Daniel Sr. glanced at me, as if he was astonished with the premise. The pallbearer, *oops*, I mean bellman, came around to open the door for Daniel Sr. and assisted him out of the limo. My limo driver assists me out as well. My personal concierge met us at the entrance of the hotel to escort Daniel Sr., and me to a lavish penthouse, which I had reserved for the weekend.

Daniel Sr. said not a word during the transition. I could feel his eyes on me every gesture I made. I wondered what was in his deceitful, selfish mind. He was probably thinking, *Oh, Raquel, this woman knows she loves her some Daniel, and I am going to get some of that money."*

Upon entering the penthouse, I could tell that Daniel Sr. was flabbergasted by the set up. Although I had grown accustomed to life's finest amenities, since winning the lottery, I was pleasantly surprised with the set up myself!

"Is there anything else we can accommodate you with, Ms. West?"

"No, that will be all," I handed the concierge a one hundred dollar bill. He thanked me profusely.

Daniel Sr. and I were finally alone. Daniel Sr. continued to look around in amazement.

"Make yourself at home, Daniel," I said. All the while I was thinking, *Enjoy heaven tonight baby, because tomorrow, your ass is going to Hell!*

The penthouse was beautifully decorated. I offered Daniel Sr. a grand tour, which he accepted graciously.

I was impressed with the array of fresh Lotus flowers through out the penthouse. The florist I'd hired did a spectacular job with the arrangement of my choice.

Daniel Sr. noticed the abundance of flowers, and dimly says, "All these flowers, this must be your favorite flower?"

"Not necessarily," I responded. "It was just what I preferred for this evening."

"What kind of flower is this?" he asked, not knowing what else to say.

"It is the lotus flower, which symbolizes estranged love," I responded.

Daniel Sr. just gazed at me with this sleazy, smirking smile. I'm sure his dumb ass did not know what the word "estranged" meant, and I was not going to waste my time telling him; unless his dumb ass was curious enough to ask me.

We commenced our grand tour of our dwelling for the evening. There was a balcony overlooking the ocean. The lounging area of the suite was renowned and inviting. The décor was lavishly done illuminating a French atmosphere with handmade, marble finished furniture, cushioned in a plush emerald tone, crafted in Paris, France. There was a beautiful replica of the *Eiffel Tower* in the middle of the room, embraced by an alluring pond of exotic fish. There was also a huge digital lasered television, mounted on the wall. There were cathedral lights dimmed perfectly to provoke the room into a romantic overtone. An entertainment bar fashioned like a "Roaring Twenties" era adorned with expensive liquors, wines, and champagnes was staged behind the Eiffel Tower replica.

The dining area comfortably seated ten people. It was an oval shaped dinette set, hand-made in Italy, with orchid wood from Europe. The table was beautifully adorned with *Chenille* china, and matching gold utensils. Colors were an alluring mauve and eggshell white. The centerpiece was a stunning arrangement of the fuchsia colored lotus flower, which was my flower of choice. I had asked the florist to be sure to have that flower everywhere in the décor, and I must admit that they did an outstanding job. There were lotus flowers all over the place.

The kitchen area was magnificently done in black, with a silver tone, and all of the amenities. There was an exotic arrangement of fruit and spring croquettes aligned in the refrigerator. Also an assortment of fruit juices I had requested for Daniel Sr., which were his favorite. He did not drink alcohol.

There were three bathrooms, each personally staged in sort of in a "patriotic" genre of colors. One of the guest bathrooms was done in an eggshell white, the second guest bathroom, all in a turquoise blue, and the master bathroom splendidly done in a Hot Red, per my request, of course. All three of the bathrooms flourished with an elite selection of perfumes, colognes, oils, lotions, soaps, and other "relaxing and soothing" essentials.

There were two bedrooms. The guest-bedroom was fabulously done in a gold tone, king size bed, also a full "meditation quarter," and entertainment area as well. The entire décor was that of majesty.

Finally, the master bedroom was done all in a dynamic red tone as I requested. *I am going to hire these interior decorators! It was exotic and sensual, but classically done!* A plushed red king-sized bed was adorned with fresh lotus flower petals There was a beautiful meditation quarter, secluded from the rest of the room. An entertainment area encompassing a digital lasered television, entertainment center fully loaded, and even a kitchenette. There were also matching lounging attire for Daniel Sr. and I.

"Damn!" Daniel Sr. exclaimed, which startled me a little. I had to keep in mind his scumbag ass was not used to any thing but sleazy hotels! After the grand tour was complete, I proceeded back into the lounging room of the penthouse, leaving Daniel Sr. alone in the master bedroom. I probably should not have left him alone; I'd hoped that his roguish ass did not steal anything!

Daniel Sr. finally emerged into the lounging area a few minutes later, as I was searching through the massive music collection in the entertaining arena. I had requested some *Patti Labelle, Whitney Houston, Yolanda Adams, Jill Scott*, and of course, *Luther Vandross* selections, and it looked like my concierge was quite obliging. I located my girl *Patti* and put on one of her CD's. *Patti* always soothed my hurting heart many times, not that it was hurting now.

"You still love you some Patti," Daniel Sr. said subtlety.

"Mmmm Mmmm," I responded. "She is a real classy woman and always soothes my spirits."

Somebody Loves You was playing gently in the midst of our conversation.

"So, Daniel, we have the entire evening to do whatever we want.

"I thought that maybe we can do some talking, or whatever you have in mind. I'm not quite ready to retire for the evening. I'd like to make this last for awhile."

"Man, you know what I want to do. I want to make love to you, all night long"

Yeah right, you can't last for ten minutes!

"Oh yeah, well we are certainly going to do that. As I said, we have all evening. I would really like to just mingle a bit and talk?" I said. "Do you have a curfew? We planned on you staying the night."

"What are you talking about? Hell no, I don't have a curfew. You know nobody runs me; I run them." Daniel Sr. eyes were that of deceit as he looked at me and said, "I'm staying here with you tonight. It might be forever, if you would let me."

This bastard is such a loser. This is pretty much what I expected of him, but I had to keep my cool and not blow my plans. I want to go off on him so bad, but now is not the time, so I took a deep breath to compose myself.

"Daniel, we discussed this earlier, and I am not playing games with you. You need to understand that I have no desire to reconcile with you in any way other than tonight. So you can deal, or not deal, but I am only betting on this evening." I said.

"Oh, so now that you got some money Raquel, you don't want to be bothered with me now?"

"Daniel, please let's not go there. **Now,** you want to be with me simply because of that. That is the reason why you are here!"

"Ahh, man, I ain't come here for this."

"Oh, yeah? Then why did you accept my invitation?"

"I told you why; you know I missed you, Raquel. You just do not want to do what I say! You just wanted to do everything your way, not giving a damn about anyone else!"

He has a lot of nerve to say that to me! How dare he? "Daniel," I said calmly, "You and I both know that is not true. I never wanted to hurt anyone, not even Leslie."

I had many reasons to hurt her slimy ass, and it was not about her taking my man. She did some devious things to me on her own; because she was so jealous of me. And I certainly never wanted to hurt Tommy, despite of all he had taken me through.

"I made a mistake Daniel! I knew better. I was so vulnerable. I was hurting, miserable, in a life sucking marriage. I knew you had not changed; did not love me, had no intention on us getting back together. You only wanted to see if you could get me back, and you used me!"

"Now, I'll admit, I did not care about anything or anyone. I just wanted to appease me and my needs at that time. I had hoped, maybe, just maybe we could have a chance or life together. I did not know how we were going to do it or when, but I was willing to take whatever risk there was. My marriage was killing me, and I just wanted to be resurrected. So, I gave into your dare, and was conned again by you."

I have to stop here, because I will surely blow my plans, and this is not my grand finale. "But, I am not mad at you, and I really do not want to talk about it anymore, okay? And do not try your bullshit ass psyche with me. It's over. Now do you want to do this, or not? We are wasting the evening with the past."

Daniel Sr. sits there dumbfounded, as if in a trance, just staring in my eyes. He took a deep breath before responding.

"Yeah, you right, man."

That's all this bastard can say? No, "I'm sorry; I never meant to hurt you?"

"Man, I know that your crazy ass ex husband is missing you and hates he messed this up with you." Daniel Sr. said. "Does he know you hit the lottery?"

"No," I reply to avoid further dialogue on the subject at hand.

"So, bad as you are, Raquel, and as good as you look, I know you got a man."

"If I had a significant other, you would not be here, now would you?" I lied.

"I don't know, man. I know you seeing somebody."

"Yes, but we have an understanding. I have been dealing with Raquel, alone. I've been doing some investing, so I've been traveling a lot. I am finally happy though."

Daniel Sr. looks at me stupidly, like he was surprised. *That's right, jackass... I don't want your tired ass!*

"So you finally divorced the maniac?" Daniel Sr. inquires, referring to Tommy.

"Yes, it was well over due. I never had any intention on reconciling with him, but I was dealing with so many transitions, and the trauma I allowed Tommy, and you as well, to inflict on me."

"Raquel, I did not inflict any trauma on you. I told you not to marry the man; you knew you still loved me."

What a sorry bastard! I could just kill him now!

"Oh, well, I am sorry about that, but the man was crazy anyway," Daniel Sr. concludes.

"So you had to give the man half of your money?"

"That's really none of your business Daniel. Besides, he can get anything from me, if he really needed it," I reply.

"Not if I was your man."

"Well, you are not my man, and I am not your woman. Don't you plan on taking care of your family with MY money?"

"I am going to take care of myself. I'm going to help Leslie out; the woman has always been there for me."

"Well then you should, Daniel. You've **been** taking care of her."

"Raquel, I don't take care of no bitch, you know that!" I do my part as a man, but the bitch better be doing her part too."

I don't even waste my time responding to this jackass!

"Raquel, how much money you plan on giving me?" the scavenger asks.

"Mmmm, I don't know. How much are you worth?" I responded with murder on my mind.

"Raquel, you know I'm worth all of it; you got millions. You can at least give me a couple of million," Daniel Sr. says.

"No problem," I responded.

Daniel Sr. just looked at me dumbfounded. This man was truly in for the surprise of his life. Did he actually think I was going to give him a dime of my money?

CHAPTER FIFTY ONE

"How are you and Leslie anyway?"

"Me and the woman fine, long as the bitch does what I say."

"You have not married her yet."

"For what? I mean, I probably will, if you won't marry me?"

"Well, I guess she finally will become *Mrs. Daniel Blake*."

Daniel Sr. glares at me with one of his cynical grins.

I got up to pour me a glass of champagne and solicited Daniel Sr. for something to eat or drink

"Can I get you something to eat or drink, Daniel?"

"Yeah, what you got? Oh, I forgot, you could get a man anything he wants."

"Mmm Mmm," I replied.

Daniel Sr. got up and proceeded to the kitchen. He opened the refrigerator and helped himself to some nectarine juice. Then he took out a tray of the spring croquettes.

"What are these? They look good."

"They are spring croquettes," I replied. "I can order you whatever you like, if that does not suit you."

"Thanks Raquel but, this is fine."

Daniel Sr. took a bite into a croquette, and licked his mouth like the dog he is. I watched him for a minute to get a response on the taste.

"This is how I am going to eat you," he said.

"Oh yeah?" I reply coquettishly.

He then slurped the juice right out of the bottle, just like the ignorant male species he is.

I walked out to the terrace with my champagne, just to embrace the beautiful scenery and meditate. Daniel Sr. is such a son of a bitch. His ass is mine! All of the pain, humiliation, emptiness, bitterness, agony, and loss he has caused me! He *will* pay for it...with his life just like I had to pay with mine.

CHAPTER FIFTY TWO

Daniel Sr. interrupts my thoughts. "Raquel, I am sorry for hurting you like I did. I was just so immature and selfish."

You still are!

"Raquel, you were the best woman I'd ever had!"

"I just did not know how to treat you." Daniel Sr. proclaims.

"You treated Leslie well." I interceded defiantly.

"Raquel, the bitch did everything I told her to do. You always bucked up at me and talked so much shit to me!"

I continued to stare into nowhere. I didn't even respond or try to justify myself. He will never get it. He is truly a lost cause. I don't know why I had loved him so much. I don't understand how I could have loved someone so passionately who just used and hurt me beyond measure. Stupidity, I guess. I was so stupid. I don't know. I've tried to understand it for so long. I've concluded so many reasons. I did not have the best childhood. I really had no mother or father, no guidance. My mother was there, but was never really a mother. I don't even know who the hell my daddy is! I know not knowing him was a huge void in my life. Rachel and I practically raised ourselves along with my two younger brothers, Carlos and Eddie. Sashe and Selena, my younger sisters were raised by my grandparents.

Daniel Sr. intruded my thoughts. "Raquel, let's go to bed, baby."

CHAPTER FIFTY THREE

I had not revealed any of the plans I had for Daniel Sr. to anyone but my two bodyguards, Sergio and Patrick. I had not even confided to Rick about this weekend I had planned. He was out of town on business, and was not expected back until next week. This gave me ample time to devise my plans for Daniel Sr. and to obliterate all evidence!

Rick and I had been dating for about six months now. He was a record promoter and a multi millionaire himself! We had met at a celebrity function in Las Vegas. After winning the lottery and dispersing money to my family and friends, I took a sabbatical to my favorite vacation spot…Las Vegas! I loved Las Vegas! The glitter, glamour, lights, celebrities, high rollers, shows, shopping, and those slot machines!

I was going to hit the casinos for a little leisure gambling. I had no need to strike it rich, because I already was. My main reason for coming to Las Vegas, other than my slot machine addiction, was to attend a star-studded gala I had heard about from some new business associates of mine.

There was a birthday party in honor of my favorite celebrity of all time, the true diva herself, *Ms. Patti Labelle*. Everyone knew that I was so crazy about my girl Patti, and I had always said that I would meet her. I was so excited!

The birthday bash was being held at the fabulous *Bellagio Hotel*, which happened to be where I was staying as well. I could not wait to attend. Of course, this was a high security level event, and I was ecstatic when my business associate was able to get me a formal invitation.

There were a lot of gorgeous, glamorous celebrity women that were there; however, I gave my competition a run for their money. I was right in their league, and my Imani red dress displayed that as well, not to mention it was fitting this sensational size nine body perfectly.

Whitney Houston, Ce-Ce Winan, Angela Bassett, everyone was there! I could not believe my eyes!

Oh my God! My favorite lady herself, *Patti Labelle*, had even approached me to comment on my dress! I forgot to breathe, but I played it off casually not to blow my cover, and calmly thanked Patti.

Is that Mr. P Diddy himself, in the flesh? Wait a minute, let me pinch myself! Am I really here, or am I dreaming? Oh my God, L.L

Cool J! Damn! I can not believe this! No, this cannot be Oprah! Look at those diamonds on her neck! This is unbelievable! Rachel is not going to believe this ! Okay, wait a minute, Raquel; calm down, keep your shit in tact! Girl, you are just as bad as these star-studded celebrities!

I cautiously took a sip of my aged brandy, and I could feel the effect through out my entire body. Or was that the effect of this gorgeous, tall, sexy, cocoa man staring at me at me from the bar? *Who the hell is that?* He was so fine!

The "mystery man" was surrounded by celebrities. Patti greeted him with a diva kiss on the cheek, and I could see that she was thanking him for coming. *Damn, is that Alicia Keys, and Beyonce? There he is again! "He" looks like Mr. L. L Cool J and Usher both! Is he an actor? If he isn't , he can damn sure play in my movie!*

Everyone was posing for pictures now. *I would love to take some snapshots with him!* Everyone scattered about now. *Thank God!* The "mystery guy" had resumed to his cascade. I pretended to be looking elsewhere, and steal another glance in his direction, and I *caught him again! Looking into my direction! I know this man is not staring at me, not with all of those beautiful women who just graced him with their presence and seemingly affection. I must look all right. Hell yeah, I do! Patti had confirmed that earlier! I subtlety returned a glare to him. What? He winked at me!*

Okay, Raquel, you can handle this! You can handle anything, so work it girl.

This was my domain and my time. I believe it and receive it! Oh my God, he is headed this way? What do I do? Please, this is not the time to lose it, Raquel! You can do this, girl. And I will! Oh my God! He is coming towards me!

I nervously retrieved my glass of brandy for a sip, and there *he* was standing in front of me! He was without a doubt, a stunning sight!

Our eyes met, and that was it! Somehow, someway, I knew I would see him again, and get to know him. Amazingly, I could smell the wonderful cologne as he made his way to me. He approached me debonairly and quite confidently.

Rick was a beautiful species of a man. He was about six foot one, a crisp mocha complexion, beautiful hair, and teeth. He appeared to be about thirty-five, just a few years my junior. I could handle that! Although he was all decked out in his Giovanni suit with matching silk shirt, my eyes seemingly had radar vision, because I could see his beautiful, masculine body through his suit. There was no ring. *Could he be gay?*

"So, I know a stunning lady like yourself is certainly not here alone," Rick said.

Not anymore! Is he talking to me? Hell yeah, Raquel... respond.

"As a matter of fact, I am; by choice, of course," I replied.

"Oh, but of course," he responded with the most alluring voice I had ever heard in my life.

He extended his hand for mine, and I happily responded. Rick had endeared my hand with a kiss. I thought I was dreaming! If there's one thing that turns me completely on about a man initially, it is when he kisses my hand. I don't know why, but when a man kisses my hand, it sends chills throughout my entire body. It displays passion, charm, and sex appeal, and I definitely welcomed all of that.

"My name is Rick Schaffer, and you?"

"Raquel," I respond coquettishly.

"So Raquel, you said you were here alone by choice. Does that mean I don't have a chance?"

Hell yeah you do!

"That's what Vegas is all about; taking chances, if I am correct," I replied.

Good one, girl, handle your business!

Rick gave me this boyish grin.

Okay, he liked that. I was on a roll.

"All right, lovely lady, I put all of my money on you," he replied.

"Did you say that you would spend all of your money on me?" I asked.

Rick let out a little chuckle. "What if I did say that?"

"Then I would ask you to join me."

Oh girl, your ass is bad! He didn't chuckle that time, but enchanted me with a beautiful smile. Rick stared into my eyes for seemingly an hour, but it was only a few seconds. Then without warning, he pulled out a chair, and joined me.

Jackpot!

CHAPTER FIFTY FOUR

Rick and I hit it off amazingly! He ordered us another bottle of *his* choice of champagne. It was *Perrier-Jouet* and I heard the server price it at $5000 a bottle! I was almost afraid to drink the shit! When the server brought the bottle of champagne over, Rick signed what appeared to be a tab.

"Raquel, I want you to try this choice champagne, which is my favorite," Rick enchanted me. "I am not attempting to get you inebriated and take advantage of you," Rick assured me.

I wish you would.

"I just want you to try the best, and by the way, I am that too," Rick assured me of his status again, with renowned confidence.

"Mmm, I bet you are," I replied sarcastically, but definitely intrigued with Rick.

I cannot believe this is happening to me. Will somebody pinch me? I know damn well I must be dreaming, or inebriated.

Rick poured me a glass of the Perrier-Jouet, and eloquently, directed the glass to my lips himself for a taste test. I must have died and went to heaven. *Wow, this stuff is good! I don't think I would pay five grand for a bottle of champagne, even though I could afford it.*

I licked my lips sensually, and Rick watched intently.

"Do you like it?" he inquired.

"Yes, it is indeed the best," I replied.

"May I pour you a glass, Rick?" I asked luminously, which seemed to intrigue him.

He cautiously leaned back in his chair and stared at me with those illustrious eyes. With an engaging smile, he nodded his head. "But of course," he replied comfortably.

I poured Rick a glass of champagne, but I dared not salute him with a taste test. My social graces were displayed with my pouring of the champagne for him, and I didn't want to appear too nurturing, not at this point.

I am innately a very nurturing woman; however, I've learned to be very cautious and in control of my life. I vowed I would never let a man have control of anything about me anymore in life. I was running Raquel now and henceforth.

Rick and I toasted, I allowed him to do the honor. I really was interested in what he would say.

"Here's to you, Raquel, and perhaps us, in the future," Rick concluded.

Wow, what a toast. To us? Is this man for real? I could not top that, so I serenaded him with my eyes, and gave him my nod of approval.

"Let the evening begin," Rick said.

"And not end," I concluded.

Rick chuckled boyishly and looked in my eyes as if he were trying to see inside of me. And then he did it again. He graciously embraced my hand and passionately kissed it, leaving an indelible mark on my heart.

CHAPTER FIFTY FIVE

Rick and I talked about a lot of things; however, I was very cautious not to spill my guts about my entire life story, not at this point. He was very classy, which I loved about a man, or anyone for that matter. Rick was a record producer, divorced for three years, and had two daughters. Rick said he had been dating, but "no one he's serious with right now."

Yeah, that's what they all say.

He told me that he had homes in New York City, Hollywood, California, Miami, Florida, and Atlanta Georgia. He had worked with *Beyonce', Alicia Keys, Usher, Patti Labelle,* and a host of others. Rick exemplified everything I ever desired in a man, thus far.

I told him that I was an entrepreneur and was involved in various lucrative business ventures.

"Yes, you certainly appear to have it together, Raquel," Rick said. "So, how is it that a sexy, intellectual, beautiful lady as yourself here alone?"

"Well, I myself am divorced, two years now," I responded.

"Hmmm, and what was your plight, if I may ask?"

"I simply could not function anymore. It was severe emotional abuse."

"Was there ever physical abuse?"

"Yes, at some point, there was."

Rick took my hand again and affectionately kissed it. "I'm sorry for the pain you experienced," he said rather empathetically.

"Any children?"

"Yes, one son."

"Just one?"

"Yes, and one grandson." I shocked him, of course.

"Grandson?"

"Yes, whom I adore."

"I can't believe you are a grandmother," Rick replied.

"I was fifteen years old when I gave birth to my son."

"Okay, so that still does not justify you being a grandmother." Rick flattered me. "I suspected you to be about thirtyish."

"Well, I am a few years older. Is that a problem?" I asked.

"Of course not. I am just amazed at how amazing you look."

"Thank you." I smiled.

I had worked very hard on toning my body and renewing my mind for the last two years. My divorce from Tommy was a major turning point in my life, and it, as well as the marriage, had truly exhausted me. So when I did finally leave Tommy, I isolated myself from all men for two years. No relationship, no sex, no nothing. I just devoted that time working on Raquel. God knows I needed that.

And it did pay off, I must say. I was forty years old and could easily pass for thirty-two. I was very proud of my accomplishments.

Rick and I continued to have casual conversation and exchanged numbers. He invited me to accompany him for the rest of the evening, but I had to stay cool. I did not want to appear easy or desperate, so I declined the invitation, for now.

I was staying at the Bellagio and was due to leave the next day; however, Rick called me at my hotel and dared me to stay a couple of more days. He offered to take care of any and all of my expenses, so how could I object? He paid my tab at the hotel and took me to the finest shops in Las Vegas and told me to get whatever I wanted! I bought *Gucci* purses, shoes, hats, attire, perfumes, any, and everything that was in-style. Rick made it clear to me that money was no object.

Where had he been all of my life? I did not reveal to him that I had plenty of money as well, I just allowed him to spend his. He knew that I was first class, and that's all he needed to know at that time.

Rick and I went to a couple of the finest restaurants in Vegas, and he even introduced me to some celebrities that he had worked with, or was currently working with.

I had been celibate for almost two years. As much as I wanted to be with Rick, I played it cool. To my surprise, he did not even pursue me sexually. But he made it very clear that he would be a part of my life and I his, and when he deemed it appropriate, we would make it happen. His tantalizing confidence really turned me on! *Where did he come from?*

I flew back home after three immaculate days with Rick, and no sex. By the time I arrived home, there was a message on my recorder from Rick, stating, "The time is appropriate now. I'll be flying down to see you in a couple of days." He went on to say that he had booked himself a room at the *Sanhedrin*, a very luxurious and expensive hotel on Miami Beach. He was going to send a limo to pick me up upon his arrival. I was so excited. Could it be that I could finally exhale after twenty-five plus years? I could not wait for those couple of days to pass so that I could see Rick again.

CHAPTER FIFTY SIX

Okay, Raquel, pull yourself together; get your self in order!
I had to go shopping. *No!* I had almost forgotten about the fabulous outfits Rick had purchased for me in Las Vegas. I only had to go get my hair done, a full body massage, a pedicure, and manicure. I called my hairstylist, my masseuse, and my manicurist, and scheduled my appointments accordingly.

Was I really ready for this, another relationship? What do I mean a relationship? Who says this would be a relationship? Rick was probably just like all of the other scumbags I've allowed myself to succumb to. I can't, and I won't, let my guard down.

After my ex husband, and me being suckered by Daniel Sr.; I had totally shut down emotionally. I was not taking any more havoc ever again from a man. I would never allow myself to love or care about a man again. I had closed my heart, and I was going to play their (men) games from now on. I would no longer be played, but would play them!

I was not going to accept anything but prime and fine. He had to be educated, intellectually stimulating, handsome, and secure within and about himself, motivated for bigger and better things, faithful, committed, sexy, and most certainly more than financially stable. And by all means, the sex had to be sustainable.

"Raquel, how was Vegas?" my sister, Rachel, asked.

"Hey, sis, it was incredible," I replied. "Girl, I met Patti Labelle!"

"What? You finally met your *Patti*, huh?"

"Yes, and it was awesome! Also, Mr. *P Diddy, Usher*, and *L.L. Cool J.*"

"Are you are kidding," Rachel responded.

"No I am not kidding, but the climax of my visit was Mr. Rick Schaffer."

"Who is Rick Schaffer?"

"My future husband," I laughed.

"Yeah, did you finally get laid?"

"No! But Rachel, he is awesome!"

"Is he a celebrity?"

"No, he is a major record producer. He introduced me to *Patti, Mr. P. Diddy, Usher, Whitney Houston*, everyone! Rachel it was unbelievable."

"Yes, well it sounds like it! I'm glad you had a ball. So what about this Rick?"

"Well, believe it or not, he'll be here in a couple of days," I replied.

"We had a ball in Vegas. He took me shopping and spent about ten grand on me!"

"What...on clothes, Raquel?"

"Yes, and he also paid my hotel tab at The Bellagio. You know I was staying in the VIP suite, which was five thousand dollars a night. In totality, he spent about thirty grand on me."

"Damn, Raquel, in just three days?"

"Yes, and when I returned home today, he left a message on my recorder that he would be here in a couple of days."

"Really, well be careful and take it slow," Rachel appeals.

"I will Rachel."

"Well, Selena and I are flying to Jamaica tomorrow for the weekend. I just wanted you to know where we would be," Rachel said.

"Please be careful and call me when you get there." I implore.

"We will."

"Love you," I concluded and hang up.

CHAPTER FIFTY SEVEN

Rick and I began a flourishing relationship, and it was incredible. *All of it!* I did not want any commitments, at least not right now. I just did not want to have to answer to anyone about anything. Rick wanted a committed relationship, but I was not quite ready for that again.

Rick understood me and where I was at in my life at the time. He respected that, and I loved that so much about him. He knew I had been through so much in my life, and I did not want any commitments with anyone. I did not want to have to give up anything of myself for any man, nor did I want to have to answer to any man. I was doing, and living only how I chose.

Rick finally accepted, and respected my feelings. We decided we would continue to see each other, always be there for each other, and we were.

Rick was the finest, sexiest, most intellectual brother I knew, and he was rich! I thought I had loved before, but loving Rick was easy. He fulfilled everything in me. I was able to expose my all to Rick, with no hesitation, embarrassment, or regrets. He was what truly liberated me. And he was what I had been yearning for all of my life!

I did not need a man to validate me or fulfill me! I just wanted a man to be a man. I wanted us to be partners in this life and conquer this world together. He should embrace his woman's liberality of being a woman. Finally, she should be able to confide in her man all of her dreams and aspirations, and he should assist her in attaining them. And yes I did believe a woman undoubtedly should reciprocate same to her man.

The stimulation I received from Rick was indeed more than sexual or physical, but it was emotional, spiritual, and finally, intellectual!

I could talk to Rick about anything, but I could not divulge to him my plans for Daniel Sr. I did not want Rick involved and this was going to be handled my way. I confided in Rick about my entire relationship with Daniel Sr. for the past twenty-five years. I had even told him about the brief affair I had with Daniel Sr. when he was released from prison after serving ten years, and how Daniel Sr. had taken advantage of my state of vulnerability, used and manipulated me again!

Rick was always upfront and honest with me. He flat out told me that I was foolish and should have known better. I knew he was right, and I had no rebuttal for that!

Rick concluded with telling me that, "No matter what, it sounds like he really took advantage of you and your love for him. You have an amazing gift of love, Raquel. I give you that. For that reason, and for the sake of your son, he should have respected you." "I am sorry he did the things he did to you, but you have got to move on," Rick says.

I laughed at Rick as if he was joking. My melancholic temperament emerged intensely, and I began to think of all that Daniel Sr. had done to me with no remorse or conscience whatsoever. I had forgiven Daniel Sr. for all that he had done to when we were supposedly a couple. But I had not recovered, despite my ongoing attempts from our second encounter and how he manipulated and used me! All I had thought about was how could I kill him and not get caught.

Rick meant a lot to me, but I was not trying to hear his reason about me needing to "move on!" I had moved on, but there was no end to my pain caused by Daniel Sr. My mind was made up, and I was still following through with my plans! Daniel Sr. will pay for everything he had done to me!

CHAPTER FIFTY EIGHT

"Okay, you go ahead, and I'll be right in," I replied.

Daniel Sr. gazed into my eyes, assessing his plan for me. *If only you knew the plans I have for you!* I was mesmerized with that thought. He gave me a nod of approval and headed to the master bedroom, and I was left alone again with my thoughts.

Daniel Sr. repulsed me and I did not know how I was going to get through making love with him! Although, the truth of the matter is, that I wanted to, just one more time. I wanted him to remember Raquel, as he made his entrance to hell!

Daniel Sr. emerged from the bedroom.

"Raquel, what are you doing? Come on in here so I can make love to you."

My mind was on nothing but Daniel Sr.'s demise, as I stared into his deceitful eyes

"Okay, baby, here I come."

He then turned and retreated back to the bedroom, as if he really had something for me.

Daniel Sr. was sitting on the edge of the bed, when I entered the room. He glared at me with this pitiful look. I did not know what his disgusting ass was reminiscing about, but I knew that it was nothing good about me.

I walked over to him, and plunged myself between his legs and kissed him passionately on his lips

"I am going to freshen up and put something on that I think you would like," I said. "Do you have any preferences?"

I went to the closet and pulled out some sexy lingerie. He gasped for a minute and I could see his arousal.

"Raquel put on that red one."

"Ahhh, the red, my favorite; I knew you would pick that one," I said.

"I know how much you love red Raquel and that's the one I want to see you in."

"I am surprised you remember Daniel how much I love red."

I am going to love seeing your red blood when this is over! Daniel Sr. revealed a smirk as if he had earned a bonus.

I progressed into the bathroom with my red lingerie to take a quick, but thorough, shower. As I anointed my body with perfume and body oils, I slipped into my lingerie. *Oh yeah... he's going to like this.*

I re-entered the bedroom and Daniel Sr. was in bed under the sheets watching television. My entrance demanded his attention, as he sat up in the bed and nodded his head approvingly.

"Wow, you look good, Raquel; I swear."

I modeled for him a few minutes, until he could not stand it anymore as he summoned me over to him.

"Come here, baby."

Daniel Sr. then turned off the television as I made my way closer to him. Our eyes were locked on each other, and for a moment, my heart pitied him. He grabbed me and started to kiss me passionately all over my face and body. Daniel Sr. appeared to be really turned on, so I let him have it.

He pulled me into the bed with him, and we caressed each other and indulged in some stimulating foreplay for about a half hour. I could feel him hardening.

"Raquel, I love you baby," he said.

I could never say that to him again.

Daniel Sr. took my panties off, and his tongue plunged inside of me like crazy! I do give him accolades for this. He does know how to swallow a woman up. He continued to absorb me passionately, and it felt good. We were both at a point of climax; I could feel it. He jumped up after what seemed like an hour and pulled off his underwear. Before I knew it, he was in me. It felt awesome. We were both moaning and groaning feverishly. Daniel Sr. surprised me this time. He survived for about thirty minutes, rather than his usual five-minute stunts.

After it was over, we were both exhausted. Daniel Sr. was staring at me as if he was actually feeling something for me.

He then surprised me when he said, "Raquel, you were the best woman I ever had in my life. I never knew how to treat you. I was young, stupid and a player. You are right; I was never on your level. You were so smart, and you had goals in life. You always took care of yourself and your business. You were so independent, and I guess I could not handle that. I was so used to the street life and being a player."

I was speechless and could only glare into his eyes with these thoughts. *You should have never played me!*

I turned away from him, with my back towards him and   dozed off to sleep satisfied.

CHAPTER FIFTY NINE

The glare of daylight awakened me as I turned to see Daniel Sr., who was still sound asleep beside me. I watched him sleep for a few minutes, and my mind wandered on all of the hurt, pain, and humiliation he had caused me for twenty-five years. *Stupid bastard; his ass got played this time!* He started to awaken, and turned to face me with sleepy eyes.

"Good morning," he said.

"Good morning. Rise and shine, baby." I replied.

I sat up on the edge of the bed and reached for my silk kimono.

The time on the clock next to me on the nightstand read 8:05 AM! My plan was scheduled to commence at 9:00 AM sharp. I had to hurry and get my ass moving.

I had requested that Patrick and Sergio be here at 9:00 AM to put my plan into motion. I'm supposed to get a phone call at 8:30 AM, alerting me that my "package"had arrived. My plan was to tell Daniel Sr. that it's the money I'd promised him. I know his ass is going to be smiling from ear to ear...but so will I.

"I am going to run and take a shower, and then if you'd like Daniel, we can have breakfast on the terrace." Daniel Sr. was on the side of the bed now.

"Come here, Raquel," he said drearily.

I walked over to him and plunged myself between his legs once again.

"Yes, Daniel?"

"I would like to have *you* for breakfast."

I'll bet you would.

"We have to get up now, Daniel. My guys will be calling momentarily to bring me your money. They will be here at nine o'clock sharp."

"Oh, okay, they're coming here with all of that money? I thought we would go to the bank or something." Daniel Sr. says.

"No, Daniel. I am flying to Paris today, and my flight leaves at noon."

"What are you going to Paris for, Raquel?"

"For business."

"You really are doing your own thing, huh?"

"I'm doing okay."

"So is this **it** between us?"

"What do you mean, Daniel? Last night was cool for me," I said deceitfully.

"Raquel, don't play games; you know I want to see you again."

"Well, give me a call, and we'll see what happens."

I'm in control now, bastard!

"I need to go shower, the guys will be here any minute," I said as I hastily run to shower.

His ass is mine! He has no idea what's getting ready to happen. I am going to make him suffer, just like I suffered for so many years.

I finished showering, slipped into my kimono, and returned to the bedroom. Daniel Sr. was on the terrace checking out the scenery.

Yeah, get a good look, baby, because your ass will never see it again!

"Daniel!" I yelled to alert him that I was out of the shower. I glanced at the clock on the nightstand again. It read 8:27 AM. *Damn!* Daniel Sr. re-entered the bedroom.

"So can I make love to you again?" he asked.

Hell no! It was pretty good last night, but it is finished!

"Daniel, I'd like to see you again, if we can work through this."

The phone rang and I walked over to answer it. Daniel Sr. was staring at me pitifully. *Don't look so pitiful now!*

"Hello."

"Ms. West?"

"Yes"

"We are prepared to bring your delivery up"

"Yes that will be fine.

"Give us a few minutes please."

"Nine o'clock sharp, okay?"

"Sure. We'll ring you again at 9:00 AM"

"Fine," I reply.

Daniel Sr. had gone into the bathroom to shower while I was engaged in conversation on the phone. *I am ready for this. Twenty-five plus years, and I am ready to give this bastard what he deserves... Death! I feel nothing for him.*

I went into the kitchen, poured myself a glass of Moët Champagne, and diluted it with a few splashes of orange juice. By the time I returned to the bedroom, Daniel Sr. was already out of the shower and half dressed. I glanced over at the clock again. I hadn't gotten dressed, because I planned on some alone time once Patrick and Sergio hauled Daniel Sr.'s ass out of here where I had instructed them to.

I had rented a cabin in an isolated location just for the occasion. It was about 60 miles from where we presently were. I had it all planned, just like a movie. Sorry for Daniel Sr.'s ass, because he would not have a happy ending.

Daniel Sr. would be taken to the location and remain there for three days. I would drive there alone and meet Patrick, Sergio, and Daniel Sr. there. I had thought about just having Patrick and Sergio knock his ass off immediately, but that was too easy. I wanted his ass to suffer.

Daniel Sr. had all of his clothes on, except for his shirt. The phone rang. *It was time!* I gave Daniel Sr. one more glance, and my heart ached for just a second, but I realized the show must go on.

CHAPTER SIXTY

Patrick held the briefcase with the money in it. He and Sergio both were ready for business, so I led my "dynamic duo" into the master bedroom. Before entering the room, I knocked on the door to summons Daniel Sr. attention.

"Yes, Raquel, I am dressed," Daniel Sr., replies unwittingly.

As I proceeded to open the door to the bedroom, I could see Daniel Sr. was sitting on the edge of the bed, fully dressed. He had no clue of the forthcoming events. As Sergio and Patrick followed me in, Daniel Sr. stood up and appeared to be somewhat startled. Sergio and Patrick both aim their guns at Daniel Sr. I had instructed Sergio and Patrick to shoot to kill if Daniel Sr. had heart enough to attempt to run.

"Get your hands up, Mr. Blake ," Sergio said sternly.

Daniel Sr. looked like he had seen a ghost. He glanced over at me and I returned his glare with no emotion.

"Last laugh, baby." I affirm.

"What's going on, Raquel? Are you going to kill me?" Daniel Sr. asks.

"Get your damn hands up now, or I will splatter your ass all over this room," Sergio said again.

Daniel Sr. realized that he had no choice, and this *was real*, so he raised his hands in the air nervously.

Patrick was behind me and emerged in front of me. He proceeded to Daniel Sr. for his much anticipated confrontation with him. I could tell Daniel Sr. was afraid and did not know what to expect next.

Patrick and Daniel Sr.'s eyes met, and Daniel Sr.'s glare was that of anguish. He then turned to me with pleading eyes, and said, "Raquel, don't do this."

I did not say a word. I seductively lit up a cigarette and took a few deep drags.

Sergio went behind Daniel Sr. and handcuffed him. I could see that Daniel Sr. was nervous and frightened with the ordeal. Sergio then pushed Daniel Sr. backwards on the bed. Daniel Sr. then gazed at Sergio and me as if he was disgusted and terrorized at the same time.

Now I had Daniel Sr. right where I wanted him! I confidently walked over to Daniel Sr. anticipating some response from him.

"Raquel, please don't kill me. I want us to have that life together we never had. I never loved anyone the way I loved you. I know I messed up. Please let me talk to you," Daniel Sr. pleaded.

I could not resist. I hated him with every bone in my body. I have pondered my mind for many years on what could I have possibly done to make him do the things he did to me!

Daniel Sr. had treated me like I was nothing to him! I could not think of one thing he ever did for me, except cause me pain. I will never forget how he connived his way back into my heart with his lies and phony promises. He took advantage of me, again, and like a fool I let him. I trusted him; I believed in him, and I loved him! He had it all planned when he was released from prison what he was going to do to me, and yes, he succeeded, as I will too with *my plans*!

Now in front of him, I glared into Daniel Sr. eyes for seemingly an hour, but it was only for a few seconds. I bent down and kissed him passionately on his lips for the second time, and whispered in his ear, *"Last laugh baby."*

"Get him out of my face," I yelled to Sergio and Patrick.

Sergio and Patrick, both with their guns drawn and aimed at Daniel Sr., lowered their guns and grabbed Daniel Sr. by his shoulder and pulled him up. Daniel Sr. was pleading with me not to let them kill him.

"Raquel, please, please don't do this! You know you will get caught!"

"If I do, your demise will be worth it," I replied.

Daniel Sr. just looked into my eyes as if *I had lost my mind. I had lost my mind!* He appeared stoical as I approached him once. again

"Daniel, I am going to give you an opportunity to live," I lied, just like he had lied to me.

"Sergio and Patrick are taking you where you will be residing for a few days."

"So hang in there, soldier," I said sarcastically.

I then gave Sergio and Patrick my nod of approval to take Daniel Sr.away.

I was finally alone. *I did it!* I lit up another cigarette and poured myself a glass of brandy. I felt good; I felt liberated. I walked out on the terrace and stared into nowhere. *Last laugh,* baby, and I began to cry.

CHAPTER SIXTY ONE

The phone rang and startled me. Damn! As I rushed to grab the phone, I noticed the time on the clock was 12:08PM! I had not realized I'd been on the terrace for two hours!

"Hello," I answered.

"Raquel? This is Alexis." *Alexis?*

Alexis was my best friend. She was as close to me as my sister Rachel and I were, perhaps even closer. I could tell Rachel anything, but I could not confide in her *these* plans, nor could I confide in Alexis!

"What's up, girl?" Alexis ask.

"Alexis, how did you know where to reach me?"

"Well, I know you said that you had some business you had to tend to and you were going to Paris, but I felt like something was bothering you. I tried calling your cell phone several times and got no answer. So, I called Sergio, and he gave me the number to where you were. You were so adamant about not revealing to me where you were going to be and what business you had to take care of. But I trust you. Whatever *business* you had, I'm sure you would have told me if you deemed necessary." Alexis said.

Damn, Alexis!

Rachel and Alexis knew me very well and could sense my distraction about something. They knew what Daniel Sr. had done to me and how it had devastated me. Even they had no idea of the pain, agony, humiliation, and guilt I had struggled with daily. No one really knew how emotionally devastated I truly was from giving so much to Daniel Sr., and Tommy for that matter, during my marriage just to have it all stripped away from me.

It was as if I was robbed of my soul. No one knew the crying inside of me that just would not stop. No matter what I did, or did not do. No one knew how angry I was at myself for allowing those two men to treat me so badly. No one had known of the suicidal thoughts that I *really* had.

My closure had been made with Tommy, but I had not reached any closure with Daniel Sr. It was time to do just that; finally, after 25 years! I was going to have closure from Daniel Sr.and I was going to make certain of that. I could not tell anyone my plans. This was something I had to do on my own.

"Alexis, girl, it's good to hear from you. Where are you calling me from?"

"Girl, Lance and I are in Jamaica, having a ball."

My girl, Alexis, she was on top now with her real estate business. I was so proud of her. She and her husband Lance had come a long way in life, too. They had been through a lot together, and certainly had weathered the storms.

Alexis got her real estate license two years ago, and was adamant about making money and becoming successful, and she was! I gave she and Lance one million dollars when I hit the lottery, and she started her own successful real estate business.

Alexis and Lance were good people, and Alexis and I clicked right away. I had only known Alexis for about five years, and I've had a lot of so called friends in my life, but she was a true friend. She had stuck with me through thick and thin.

My ex husband Tommy was so jealous and did not approve of any of my friends. I had lost a few friends because of his ignorance, and them just not wanting to deal with Tommy.

But Alexis *made* Tommy like her, or pretend to like her. Tommy did not really like anyone who was affiliated with me. Alexis knew just how to handle him, and I loved that about her. Her husband, Lance, was such a good guy. He believed in taking care of his family, and was like a brother to me. They both meant so very much to me. I was so happy I was able to share some of my lottery winnings with them to let them know how special they were to me and a very important part of my life.

"What? Alexis, you did not tell me you guys were going there."

"We just went on a whim."

"Where is my godson?"

Alexis and Lance's three year old son Xane was my godson.

"My sisters have him. I talked to him on the telephone today; I miss my baby. You should have heard how well he was talking, Raquel."

"I could imagine Alexis!"

"How long have you been there?"

"Two days. We are staying another couple of days, and then we are flying back home. Lance and I needed some time together alone. I've been so busy, and so has Lance. Raquel, I sold two houses last week, and you will not guess to who!"

"Who, Alexis?"

"I sold one to *Iylana Vanzant* in Atlanta, and one to *Simone*, in LA."

"What? Girl, I know that netted you a huge commission."

"Yes, two hundred thousand!"

"What? That is awesome, Alexis!"

"So, Raquel, since you are my best friend and "advisor," I want you to accompany me to the closing for *Simone* which is in two weeks."

"Sure, Alexis, you know I'll be there."

"I will book your flight next week, and I will need to know where to pick you up," Alexis said.

"Also, is there going to be anyone accompanying you Raquel?"

"No, not at this point, Alexis."

"All right, just let me know if you change your mind, Raquel."

"I will call you the beginning of the week Alexis."

"Ok, and are you sure you are ok, Raquel?"

"I am fine Alexis. I'll talk to you real soon."

"Ok, love ya!"

"I love you too Alexis," I conclude, and hang up.

CHAPTER SIXTY TWO

I have to kill him! I think to myself en route to the cabin where Daniel Sr., Patrick, and Sergio were.

He must die! He just stood there and watched me die slowly inside for all of those years. Why should I pity his sorry ass? I hate him! Yet, I loved him so passionately, once.

I did not blame anyone for my bad decisions. I do not even blame Daniel Sr. I did what I did, and I make no excuses for myself about that. I realize I made some very poor choices. And I am not soliciting any pity from anyone. But Daniel Sr. took advantage of my vulnerability and me. He reaped on the feelings he knew I still had for him. He knew what I suffered loosing Clyde, Daniel Jr. going to prison, and all of the havoc Tommy had taken me through! Daniel Sr. was only concerned about himself, like he always had! I also tried to help him. Yes, I knew better, but evaded all rationale and succumbed to his tactics once again. I did not deserve what Daniel Sr. had done to me, and he was going to pay!

I finally made it to the cabin. It was really secluded here. No sign of life other than this cabin. Just the location I'd needed to carry out my plans!

Sergio greeted me at the door with a smile, and kissed me on my cheek. As I made my entrance inside, I noticed Daniel Sr. in a chair handcuffed. Patrick was on guard sitting in a chair pulled along side Daniel Sr.

I had told Sergio and Patrick to make sure Daniel Sr. was comfortable, but he had to remain restrained at all times. Daniel Sr. appeared to be fine, except his face was really solemn as he glared at me upon my arrival.

I made my way to a little breakfast bar centered in the middle of the cabin. I had Patrick and Sergio pick up some food and champagne to sustain us while we were here. I poured me a glass of champagne and cautiously took a sip as I returned to face off with Daniel Sr. Sergio was already ahead of me and lit a cigarette for me which I proceeded to take a nice drag.

"Do you know why you are here?" I asked Daniel Sr. sarcastically.

His head lifted slowly as he glared at me with pitiful eyes.

"Yes, because I hurt you." He then dropped his head, and repeated,

"I hurt you," as if he was speaking to himself.

I gazed at Daniel Sr. for a few minutes in utter disgust! My mind rehearsed the pain, humiliation, unstoppable tears, and restless nights. I tried to think of something, *anything* good about Daniel Sr., but honestly, I was unable to conjure up any decent thought of him.

"You are so pathetic!" Do you know that? You are indeed the vilest individual I have ever known! Do you see what you've done to me, what you have made me? You selfish bastard, all you had to do was go on your merry way like a decent, moral man for once in your life. I would like for you to tell me what I did to you in the twenty five years that I've known you, not to mention have your first born son, for you to treat me the way you treated me and do the things you did to me."

Daniel slightly held his head up and his eyes pierced mine again.

"Raquel, you act like you did not do anything!" he yelled.

Oh, this bastard still has a little heart, but that was the wrong answer. This time I slapped his ass in his pretty face as hard as I could. At least that was his delusion of himself. He had pissed me off!

"You are one sorry piece of crap," I said to Daniel Sr. "I did nothing to you, ever, to warrant your treatment of me!

Daniel Sr. just stares at me as if he had seen a ghost and I returned the same to him.

He raised his head, and I was amazed that there were actually tears rolling down his cheeks. But I really didn't care. He could cry blood, and he will. He never cared about the tears I cried, day and night.

"I was young, dumb, and weak. I thought I had it going on," Daniel Sr. finally responded. "I treated you bad, real bad, and I did not give a damn. I just wanted to do what I wanted to do, but I did love you and my son," Daniel Sr. says.

I stared into Daniel Sr.'s pitiful eyes, and thought about how trifling he really was!

"Love! How could you even think about fixing your mouth to say that you loved my son and me? All of the pain, hurt, humiliation, insensitivity, unconscionable things you did to us. Of course, me more so, but when you did them to me, you did them to him. So, Daniel, you loved us when you cheated on me hundreds of times, beat on me, disrespected me! You loved me when you would leave Daniel Jr. and me for days at a time to go on your scout tramp sabbaticals, while I had to work and go to school? I would pace my floor at night, unable to sleep, because I was hurting so badly! I was not worried about you, because I knew just where you were, with a tramp, as usual! You made all of these babies with these women you were dealing with! So you were loving me when you left me for a tramp with not even a middle school education? Although *that*, I understand because you never had one yourself. You had so much money and would not give me a dime to take care of our son, but had no problem taking care of tramps and their families! So you loved me after you were living it up with your new tramp? When I asked you for money for our son, you told me the only way I could get some money from you was that I drive some drugs for you out of the state! You did not give a damn about my livelihood or your son! You sorry son of a bitch! How dare you say you loved us?"

"Hit his ass!" I yelled to Sergio.

Sergio readily obliged, and slapped Daniel Sr. across the back with a belt.

Daniel Sr. screamed in agony, like the wimp he was!

"Did that hurt, Daniel?" I asked sarcastically. "Now you know how I've felt for so long! Remember when you used to beat me with belts Daniel!" I screamed.

Daniel Sr. slowly held his head up. He glared up at me like he was going to erupt, and said unwillingly, "Yes, Raquel, I remember, and I am sorry!"

"I am sorry too Daniel for what I have to do!" I conclude.

"Daniel, I want you to do everything I instruct you, which of course, you have no choice, now do you?"

"No, I do not," Daniel Sr. said rather sarcastically.

"I am going to have Patrick remove your handcuffs, because I need your hands free for a moment. Please be reminded, that if you try anything that is not in accordance to my plan, you will fail. Do you understand, Daniel?"

"Yes, Raquel, I understand," Daniel Sr. replied pitifully.

I summoned Patrick over and requested that he take the handcuffs off of Daniel Sr. Patrick looked at me hesitantly, but dared not question my ulterior motive for my request.

Sergio, in the meantime, was standing guard as he was so well paid to do. Patrick removed Daniel Sr.'s handcuffs as Daniel Sr. raised his head and pleadingly glared into my eyes. I decided to taunt Daniel Sr. a little more.

"Daniel, how do you think I look?"

"Sexy, beautiful," he replied.

"Am I enticing to you," I interrupted.

"Yes, always," he responded again pitifully.

I walked over to Daniel Sr., and I could see the perplexity in his face as I made my way to him. I bent down and whispered in his ear,

"I want you to remove my panties, *without* touching my skirt. I want you to peel them off, like you are peeling the skin off of a banana." I laughed wickedly into his ear. Daniel Sr. stared at me again, as if I had lost my mind.

"Now!" I said demandingly.

Daniel Sr. cautiously raised his hand under my skirt as I stood in front of him. Sergio and Patrick stared in the background as if they were astonished, and I halted my hand towards them to assure them that I had this under control. Daniel Sr. continued nervously with his attempt to remove my panties, while staring into my eyes, and again cautiously slipped both of his hands up my skirt. He licked the sweat off of his lips as if he was getting ready to have a treat. He finally clung on to my hips and slowly removed my panties even though his hands were shaking like a winter leaf. He held my panties as if they were a piece of gold.

I wanted to laugh. After the delicate task was over for him, I stared into his eyes, in which he returned a glare to me as if to say, "Do I get any points for that?" Of course, my answer would be an emphatic, "NO!" On the contrary, he just expedited his impending death, because his methodical success on removing my panties really felt good.

Sergio and Patrick both were wiping the sweat off of their foreheads. I smiled to myself and imagined their thoughts. I returned my attention to Daniel Sr., as I pierced his eyes with mine. I thrust my left leg over his lap, and I could feel his entire body shake. I then placed my right leg over his lap, and I was sure I felt something wet? I bent down and passionately licked Daniel Sr.'s left earlobe, and whispered into his ear.

"Are you afraid of me?"

Daniel Sr. glared into my eyes, and responded,

"Right now, I am," he replied.

I smiled as I returned his glare, and slowly got up.

"Sergio!" I yelled. "Put Mr. Blake's handcuffs back on him." I retrieved my panties from Daniel Sr.'s lap and slipped them slowly back on. Sergio nervously, but successfully, handcuffed Daniel Sr. and returned to his post.

Daniel Sr. continued to stare at me with pleading eyes as I returned to my front row seat.

"Now, where were we, Daniel?" I asked tauntingly. "Daniel, are you afraid of dying?"

Daniel Sr. continued to glare into my eyes, as if he was asking for mercy.

"I'm worried about how I will die," he responded as he dropped his head.

"Well, Daniel, how do you want to die?" I asked unemotionally.

"I don't want to suffer," Daniel Sr. replied.

I began to laugh uncontrollably, and I caught Daniel Sr. watching me.

"You do not want to suffer?" I asked as if he was joking. Daniel Sr. did not say a word.

"Do you think I've suffered?"

"Yes, I can see that you suffered, and I am so sorry," he said almost convincingly. "I had no idea of what I put you through until now."

"You think you have a pretty good idea of how much I suffered, Daniel?"

"No, apparently not."

I looked into his eyes hoping to see some genuinely, but I could not.

"You are correct; you have no idea, Daniel! As much as you think you are suffering now, it by no means is comparable to my suffering inflicted by you."

Daniel Sr. continued to glare into my eyes stoically.

"You see, Daniel, you broke me. You broke me emotionally, physically, and as you can see, maybe even a few mental cracks!" I laughed viciously.

Sergio and Patrick were staring at me cautiously; I assumed that they were stunned by my words, and the previous event. I returned a reassuring glare to Sergio and Patrick to ensure them that I was indeed still in control.

"Daniel, all you had to do was be a man about it. The problem for me was not you loving me back, but you should have been honest with me. You should have never, ever infiltrate my life again. After ten years, you knew what I had been through, yet you still took advantage of me. I was in a miserable marriage. I was already hurting desperately, and you knew that! I would have helped you out in any way I could, without the lies and manipulation! You did not have to lie to me. I was not someone you'd just met! We had a history! I gave you your first son! "Didn't you ever give a damn about that? Of course not, why in the hell would I think you would?" You never were there for him anyway, because you are a wimp! You used me for your own well-being, with not one ounce of conscience of what it would do to me. What is even more appalling to me is that you did it intentionally and willingly. Remember what you told me along with all of the other lies? We would be together; you were going to leave Leslie; you still loved me, and so on. What did you say to me, Daniel?"

Daniel, Sr. glared up at me dumbfounded and with pleading eyes again.

"I don't know what I said," he replied as if he had given up his fight.

"I will never forget it! It's like a tape recorder in my mind and heart, so how in the hell, you don't remember it?" I yelled.

"You remember asking me for my money, don't you?" You remember taking it from me, don't you?"

"Yes, Raquel."

"You told me that someone was going to be hurt. Don't you remember saying that to me, Daniel?" "You pretended like that likely outcome grieved you!" "I had a lot at stake as well, remember? Therefore, you hurt me willingly and intentionally, you son of a bitch!"

I paused for a few minutes to collect myself, and Daniel Sr. retreated as if he was trying to redeem himself.

"Raquel, I messed up! You are right; I was weak. I was a dog! I thought I had it going on, but never had shit! I never, ever stopped loving you or Daniel Jr., never. You're right; I wanted my cake and eat it too. When I got out, I had nothing! I was desperate, and needed help! I was not trying to use you Raquel! I had nowhere to go Raquel!"

"You should have kept going, you son of a bitch," I angrily stated.

"How dare you use me and take my money to appease your miserable, well-deserved, if I may add, crisis! You ruined me, you son of a bitch. You took whatever piece of sanity I had left! I was in a desperate situation myself, dealing with my problems in my marriage, wanting to leave it, but committed to making it work. Not to mention having to deal with unresolved issues with *you*, when your ass re-surfaced," I yelled. "You should have never thought about betraying me again, after all of the shit you'd put me through. I never deserved any of it!" I continued to yell. "But you had to use and humiliate someone, and I guess I was the likely target. Was that it, Daniel?"

"No, Raquel," Daniel, Sr. replied.

"Okay, Daniel, this conversation is over," I said.

Daniel Sr. exhaustingly dropped his head. I retreated into a few moments of solitude, attempting to regain my composure. *Can I think of any happiness, decency, respect that he imparted in my life,"* I wondered, trying desperately to redeem him, but my answer, unwavering, is an emphatic *"NO!"*

Daniel, Sr. continued to hold his head down, and I couldn't believe that he was actually whimpering like the dog he is! *Surely, it's not because he is sorry for what he did to me, but he's sorry that his trifling ass is no longer in control, but Raquel is!*

"Daniel, you've failed at redeeming yourself," I say stoically, and mean it!

Daniel Sr. finally held his head up, and I could see his exhaustion. His eyes were bloodshot red, and his face was somewhat pale and pitiful. He looked as if he had just given up. He glares into my eyes, and tears slowly, emerge from his eyes.

Daniel Sr. says dementedly, "Raquel, I am so sorry for hurting you the way I did."

His tongue licked the tears from his mouth. I returned a glare into his eyes and did not respond at all. *Then it happened... I lost my grip!*

Daniel Sr. had succeeded in manipulating my heart to feel for him again, but just for a few minutes. I tried desperately to fight it, but the tears began to roll down my cheek and I could not stop them. I was so angry with myself. I never, ever wanted him to see me shed another tear, but he got me, again. I stood up, embarrassed, because I'd let down my guards. I had to replenish myself.

I paced the floor a few times, continuously drying my eyes. I could not believe that I allowed myself to cry. Sergio and Patrick, still standing guard, both glared at me as if they wanted to console me. Sergio began to walk towards me, but I held my hand up for him to stop, and he retreated back. I just needed that moment to myself. I pulled myself together outwardly, but inwardly, the pain was still prevalent. I slowly walked back over to Daniel, Sr. still teary eyed , and I sat back into my chair.

Daniel, Sr. held his head up again, and pierced my now red eyes.

"I am so sorry for what I did to you, how I treated you. I did love you though. Raquel, I just got caught up in the game."

I listened to him with no emotion at all, and then I calmly responded, "Daniel, you had won the game, you should have took your winnings and continued on. I never loved another man the way I loved you, and you knew that. You used that to slither your way back into my life for your own, selfish desires. You knew what I was going through, the kind of person I was, compassionate, caring, and would have done anything to help you because I still cared for you. You used me. You conned me. I pleaded with you, because after you got what you wanted from me, you simply gave me your ass to kiss. I trusted you. I was so afraid of being hurt by you again. I risked everything in my life for you. I wanted to believe you, I had no choice."

Daniel Sr. just shook his head while I talked. I got up and pulled myself together. *I was done!*

"Raquel, can't you ever forgive me?" Daniel Sr. pleaded as I slowly walked towards the door. I turned around to answer him for *his* final time.

"No, I cannot forgive you, Daniel. It is finished," I said, and exited to return home.

CHAPTER SIXTY THREE

I decided to let Patrick and Sergio do what they did best and *finish the job* at the cabin. I was certain that I wanted it done, but at the end, I could not do it myself. I told Patrick and Sergio I did not want Daniel Sr. to suffer and for them to notify me when the job was done.

As I made my way to my front door, I could smell *his* cologne upon entering the house. Rick was here! I sure needed him to be, after what I had just gone through.

Rick emerged from the terrace looking as gorgeous as ever. He was wearing a pair of Versace jeans embraced with a fitted Versace white oxford shirt, fine as ever!

"Hey, sexy, how long have you been here?" I asked.

"About an hour."

Rick walked over to greet me. As Rick approached me, he noticed the redness in my eyes. "Raquel, are you okay?" He asked while lovingly stroking my face.

"Yeah, I'm fine," I replied, trying to hide a tear that surfaced out of nowhere.

"Raquel are you sure you are okay?"

"I'm fine, baby," I replied.

A slight regression of my previous atmosphere caused a tear to trickle down my face. Rick lifted my head up toward the light and glared into my eyes. He bent down and kissed my tears. I was shaking at that point.

Rick took my hand, stared into my eyes, and said, "We can talk now, or we can talk later."

"Later," I said.

Rick nodded with approval, and led me into the master bedroom.

THE END! SMOOCHES!